Deep Heat

A Romantic Comedy
By Stacey Broadbent

Deep Heat

Deep Heat

A Romantic Comedy
By Stacey Broadbent

Contents

Dedication

To all the people of the world.
You are beautiful just the way you are.
Don't let anyone dim your sparkle.

Glossary

Deep Heat is set in New Zealand, so some NZ slang terms have been used. These are not errors, it's just how we speak over here.

Deep Heat	A warming cream to aide muscular pain
Chip shop	Fish and chip shop
Haere mai	Come here
Auē	An expression of astonishment To cry, howl, or groan
Anō te pai	That's excellent! Fantastic!
Kia ora	Greeting, hello
Koru	A spiral shape based around an unfurling silver fern frond
Rā whānau koa	Happy birthday

Deep Heat

Chapter one

"I swear I'm not a pervert, doc. I, um, slipped?" It comes out as a question rather than a statement, and one that makes me sound guilty as sin, because I am.

Doctor Mitchell raises her brow as she continues scrawling notes on her board.

Like a crazy person, I continue talking. "I mean, it's just not right. A woman of my age shouldn't find herself in this kind of position." A nervous laugh escapes my lips as I pick at the edge of the sheet I'm lying on. "Of course I know that's not what it's for, it's just… well… the shape is rather phallic-looking, especially after consuming a few wines…" I trail off, brushing my hands down the sheets to smooth them, looking anywhere but at her. "There should be some kind of warning label, you know?"

Doctor Mitchell lowers the board, and I don't have to look at her to know she's raising her brows. I can *feel* the judgement pouring off her in waves. "I understand what you're saying, Marianne, I do. But it says quite clearly on the box, 'for external use only'." She holds the package out and shows me the fine print right there on the front. Her eyes widen as she shakes her head, the hint of a smile playing on her lips. At least someone is amused by this.

Squinting, I bring it right up close. "Well, would it hurt them to use a larger font? I mean really, who can read that tiny writing?" I toss the box on the table with a huff, folding my arms across my chest and staring at the wall. Perhaps it's time I give in and start wearing my glasses all the time and not just for the morning crossword and sudoku puzzles in the paper. I pull my lips into a thin line as I picture that, then quickly shake my head. No. It's bad enough I have grey hairs trying to take over my head (and other areas that shall remain nameless), I refuse to give in and wear those ugly things any longer than necessary. I don't care that Doctor Cavanagh suggested I do so, they make me look 60 instead of the spritely 39 that I am. So the lines blur a little when I'm reading street signs, and my TV planner looks like a grey box of fuzz, I can still see the important things. Mostly.

Doctor Mitchell smiles, placing her hand on mine. "It's perfectly normal to want to… experiment with things, but maybe next time find something a little less… heat inducing."

I nod, bringing both sides of the pillow up to encase my face and hide my shame. This is not how I saw my Saturday night playing out. Curse that Jamie Oliver and his seductive ways. There's something about a man who knows his way around a kitchen that really gets my motor running, only this time, I let it run a little too far. "In my defence, I thought the lid was on properly. But I'm sure you see this kind of thing all the time though, right?" The hope that laces my voice is almost as embarrassing as being admitted to hospital for getting a little too frisky with myself. I bet they'll all be having a laugh about this around the water cooler when I'm gone.

"Oh, I've seen my fair share of things lodged where they shouldn't be, but I can tell you, this is a first for me."

"It is?" I swallow. Maybe I *am* a pervert.

"Look." The bed dips as Doctor Mitchell leans her hand on the bed beside me. "I'm not here to judge. It might be the first time, but it certainly won't be the last. You'd be surprised what people 'fall' on in all their naked glory." She reaches up to grab a pair of gloves. The sharp slapping sound of rubber on skin reverberates through the room, and I unintentionally clench.

"Ooh, my lord!" My cheeks heat as I feel the tube lodge itself even farther inside, and another squirt of the cool yet burning cream escapes. Why didn't I check the lid was on securely? I mean, it's like 101 of sex ed; make sure whatever you're inserting doesn't have any loose bits that can fall off and get lost somewhere inside the matrix that is my vajayjay.

Doctor Mitchell grabs a speculum from her instrument tray, and I swear it's the biggest one I've ever seen. "You know the drill. Knees up, legs apart."

I follow her instructions, staring up at the ceiling when a thought hits me, and I clamp my legs firmly together. "Wait!"

She stops, her weapon coming to a halt on my shins. "There's nothing to be scared of. It's just like a smear."

Only it's not, is it? "I don't know about you, doc, but there's not normally a search and rescue involved in my smears." To her credit, she bites her lip to stop herself from what I'm sure would have been a laugh at my expense. I get it. I'd laugh too if it wasn't happening to me.

"No, I suppose not." She straightens, meeting my gaze. "Here's what I'm going to do. I'm going to go in with the speculum so I can see what I'm dealing with. The end of the tube will have sharp corners and I'm going to need some room to pull it back out without scratching the walls or expelling any more *Deep Heat* into you."

Internally cursing myself for my stupid actions, I throw an arm across my eyes and nod as I let my legs fall apart. "Okay, doc. Do what you have to."

"Right. Going in now." There's a cold bite of metal against my skin and, once again, I clench. It's like a kneejerk reaction. "You're going to have to relax, Marianne. I can't do much while you're tense like this."

"Easy for you to say, you're not the one with fire-breathing lotion coating your temple of doom now, are you? Oh God!" My head jolts from the pillow, my eyes wide. "What if you push it in farther with that thing? What if you can't get it out?" Clutching my chest, I throw myself back onto the bed, my breath coming in quick succession. "I can't live my life with a tube of *Deep Heat* forever lodged down there. I'll never be able to have sex again!" The walls seem to be closing in on me, and I still can't catch my breath.

"Marianne? I need you to calm down." Doctor Mitchell places her weapon of torture on the tray again, moving around to my side. "Look at me." I do as I'm told, though I can't seem to get the air I need into my lungs. "Marianne, you're having a panic attack. I need you to breathe. Nice and slow now, with me." She takes a breath in through her nose and out through her mouth. "With me, Marianne."

I try. Lord knows I try, but black dots dance before my eyes, and the last thing I hear is, "Shit."

Chapter two

Stretching my arms above my head, I blink my eyes open against the harsh light. Did I fall asleep under the heat lamp in the bathroom? It wouldn't be the first time that's happened after a few too many vinos.

"Ah, there she is," a husky voice says from somewhere beside me, and I jolt upright, coming face to face with a silver-haired fox in a crisp, white doctors' coat. He has one of those panty-dropping smiles that make the sides of his eyes crinkle, and I just about melt into them. There's a hint of stubble on his jaw, enough for me to wonder what it would feel like against my fingers (and other places). Where did this dreamy man come from, and what is he doing in my bathroom? "How are you feeling?"

I blink, the realisation of the situation sinking in. I'm still in the hospital, wearing one of those hideous gowns that don't do up at the back. My legs are in stirrups and there's a half-empty tube of *Deep Heat* lying on the table beside him, which can only mean one thing; Doctor Hottie has been inside my hooha. He's traversed the plains no man has set foot in for at least three years.

I don't know whether to be turned on or mortified. I mean, I haven't even waxed!

My eyes widen, and I quickly clasp my hands across my lower half, as if covering myself is going to rewind the tape and stop him from seeing me in my awkward predicament. Of course, that just opens the back of my gown, exposing the rest of my body to this extremely gorgeous man who doesn't even bat an eye as I fumble to gather the material together.

"Uh, where's Doctor Mitchell?" I manage to say, my voice rising to an octave that could surely summon dogs. "She was here a minute ago." My eyes dart around the room in search of her. Don't get me wrong, it's always a pleasure to wake up next to an attractive man, but I prefer to be wearing something a little more flattering, and a little less like a shapeless sack. I also like to be of sound mind when a man is servicing the downstairs area. I mean, it's just common decency not to fall asleep.

Doctor Hottie stands, wrapping his warm hands around my wrist to check my pulse. "Easy there, Marianne. We don't want you having another panic attack. Doctor Mitchell was called out to an emergency, so I'm filling in for her." He smiles, and I swear I hear birds sing.

"Oh, okay. So, ah, you're just supervising then? You didn't…" I pull my lip between my teeth as my eyes flick to the offending tube then down to my barely covered crotch.

His cheeks colour and a tiny smirk graces his lips before he clears his throat, meeting my gaze. "I'm afraid I did." He nods.

"Oh!" An almost hysterical giggle bursts from my lips, and I quickly slap a hand across my mouth. I don't know why I'm laughing because it's not funny. The first time a good-looking man comes face to face with the bearded clam in years, and I don't even get a happy ending. What a rip!

He holds his hands up, palms out. "No judgement here. Each to their own," he says as if it's an everyday occurrence. "You might experience a little tenderness for the next few days. I'd recommend abstaining from intercourse until that has subsided."

I snort, shaking my head. "Like that's going to be a problem. If I was having intercourse, I wouldn't be in this position in the first place." My eyes widen as I slap a hand across my mouth.

Did I just say that out loud? To the hot doctor?

His eyebrows shoot up, but to his credit, he doesn't say a thing, just nods and grabs the curtains surrounding the bed as he clears his throat. "I'll ah, leave you to get changed." He nods again, like the professional he is, but I'm sure I can see amusement in his eyes.

Once the curtains are pulled, I slip off the side of the bed, noticing there's still a bit of heat radiating from my nether regions. I'm not sure if it's the effects of the *Deep Heat* still coating my insides, or if it's another thing entirely. That thing being the silver-haired man with the crinkles around his eyes.

Chapter three

"You did not!" Susan gasps, covering her mouth with her hand as she tries not to laugh at my expense.

"Unfortunately, I did." I shake my head as I carry the plate of freshly baked cookies to the coffee table, where we're set up. After last night's debacle, I'd thrown myself into the only thing that makes me feel sane; baking. "I wouldn't recommend it." She stares at me with wide eyes and a shaky lip, and I can tell she's about to burst. "My hooha will never be the same again," I sigh, dropping my chin to my chest and peeking up at her through my lashes. Here it comes, in three, two, one…

Susan presses her lips together in one last attempt to hold it in, but her laugh forces its way through her lips, spraying wine droplets all over me in the process. This only makes her laugh more.

"You know, one of these days it's going to be you doing something stupid, and when that day comes—" I raise an eyebrow at her as she snorts, "—I will laugh my arse off too." I grin. Leaning forward, I swipe a napkin from the table and blot myself dry. Thank God it's a white wine and not red like last time. My eyes fall to the couch cushion beside me, knowing that underneath is a permanent ruby stain from our last girls' night.

"Therein lies your problem," Susan chokes out as she fans her face with her hand. "*I* don't do stupid things." She waggles her eyebrows and takes another mouthful of her wine as she helps herself to a cookie. We both know she's full of shit. Of the two of us, she's the one who is out on the prowl most weekends, while I'm tucked up at home, trying out recipes I've seen on the TV, or reading a good book.

I raise an eyebrow at her. "Okay fine, but I don't get caught doing it when I do." She snorts. "Although maybe I should." She purses her lips in thought. "I mean, if it could get me a date with a hunky doctor, I'll do some stupid shit. Just point me in the right direction." She leans back, taking a bite of her cookie and humming with satisfaction.

"Please, like you need any help in that department." I roll my eyes. Susan is a stunner. For as long as I've known her, and that's a long time, she's always had men falling at her feet. She could have the pick of the litter, so to speak. In fact, I wouldn't be surprised if she'd already banged Doctor Hottie. She *does* have a thing for men in uniform.

Placing her hand to her chest in mock outrage, she sucks in a breath. "I'll have you know, I haven't had sex in three weeks. Three weeks!" She holds up three fingers to really drive her point home. "That's gotta be some kind of record."

Now it's my turn to snort. "Oh, honey, you have no idea. Try three *years*." I lean back against the couch, out of wine-spitting distance.

"Years?" she shrieks as she scoots to the edge of her chair. "As in thirty-six months?"

I shrug. "Give or take."

She frowns, taking hold of my hand. "Are you… okay?" Her eyes flit to my crotch and back up again, and I bark out a laugh.

"God, Suz, of course I'm okay! Just because I haven't had sex in three years, doesn't mean it's not working. It's a choice. Sex isn't everything, you know."

Her frown turns to a look of pity. "If you think that, then I feel sorry for the men you've slept with in the past, because they clearly don't know what they're doing. Sex *is* everything, if it's done right." She grabs her phone and starts swiping her finger across the screen. "We need to get you laid, stat."

"Oh no we don't!" I lunge for the phone, but she holds it out of my reach. "Doctor Hottie said no sex until I'm all healed." I fold my arms across my chest with a satisfied smirk. "You can't go against the doc's orders."

She purses her lips, letting her phone drop to her lap with a sigh. "Okay fine. But once that—" she waves a finger through the air at my nether regions, "—is all kosher, you're getting back out there and on the proverbial horse."

"I don't know…"

"Well I do. That whole *Deep Heat* thing was a cry for help, and I am like your coochie's fairy godmother.

Lord knows it needs it." She slumps back on the couch muttering, "Three years," under her breath.

Chapter four

"Morning, Marianne. Is that more of those kickass chocolate muffins you have there?" Daniel asks as I walk into the office.

"It sure is." I hold the tray out to him, and he helps himself to two, taking a large bite of one straight away.

"Mmm. Awesome as always. You could make a killing with these, you know?" He closes his eyes as if savouring the taste. "Plant yourself outside the pub on a Saturday night, and you'd be creaming it."

My cheeks heat at his colourful use of words, and I have to remind myself he doesn't know what happened to me; it's just a figure of speech. "Ah, thanks. I'll keep that in mind."

"How was your weekend? You get up to much?" he asks, shoving the other half of the muffin into his mouth.

"Oh, you know, the usual." My inner voice snorts as I continue past to my desk, setting the tray on the ledge above my computer. I would die of mortification if he, or anyone else from the office, found out about my escapades on Saturday night. It's bad enough Susan knows, especially now that she's hellbent on setting me up with some sex stallion from a website. I just don't know how it can be safe, what with all those scammers and catfishers out there. How do you know you're actually talking to a legitimate person and not a robot? Call me old-fashioned, but I think I prefer the way things used to be before this social media palaver came along. What's so wrong with meeting someone at the grocery store or the library?

They're all too busy with their noses in their phones to bother looking up and striking up a conversation, that's what.

Don't get me wrong, I'm still hip and with it, I think, but I just don't see the need to be glued to my phone like it's my only lifeline in the world. Oh god, that's exactly what an old person would say. No matter how hard I try to clutch onto the days of my youth, they keep slipping through my fingers like that disgusting slime stuff that's all the rage these days.

Maybe Susan is right. Maybe I do need to get up on that horse again, and if using one of those websites she's so fond of is how it's done nowadays, then I guess I'd better start practising my duck face.

"Are you okay?" Daniel asks as he hands me an overstuffed file with a frown on his face. "You look like you just sucked a lemon."

I pull my lips into a straight line and nod, feeling the heat rise from my chest through to my face and onwards. I don't have to look in a mirror to know my cheeks will be a lovely shade of crimson. It's the curse of a pale complexion and red hair. "Mmhmm. Fine and dandy."

"Right." He draws out the 'I', shoving his hands in his pockets and rocking back on his heels. "Anyway, Mark wants these typed and on his desk by the end of the day."

I flick through the file to avoid making eye contact. "Sure, no problem." I switch on the computer and busy myself with organising the desk how I need it for the day, but he continues hovering, like he's waiting for something. "You need something else?" I ask, finally turning my gaze to meet his. I knew I should've made a double batch of muffins.

"Ah," he clears his throat, his face flushing as he rakes a hand through his hair with a grin. "It's just that I um, saw you…" he gestures to my face, "your profile." He holds his tongue between his teeth in an odd sort of leer that just seems creepy, and I wonder if he's been smoking out back. Probably why I have no idea what he's on about.

"My… profile?"

The grin spreads wider. "Yeah, on HookUp.com."

"What?" I practically screech as I scoot backwards in my seat. "What did you just say?"

His grin falters as he takes a step back, peering over his shoulder. "Uh, that I saw your profile on HookUp.com," he stammers, "and I just wanted to say I think it's cool, ya know? For someone your a—" He stops himself, tugging at his collar. "I just think it's cool is all."

I know what he was going to say; that it's cool for someone my age to be on a site like that, looking for a 'hook up' as the name suggests. I'm going to kill Susan when I see her next.

Lowering my voice, I glance around the room. "Does anyone else know?"

"Oh," he nods, rocking on his heels again. "You want it kept on the DL? No worries." He zips a finger across his lips. "Your secret is safe with me. But, ya know, it's cool though." He shrugs. "It's not like anyone can see it unless they're looking to hook up too. So it's all gravy."

"They can't?"

"Nah, there's all this background security shit. If you're going to be on an app, that's the one to be on for sure." He grins, bouncing a fist against my desk. "Happy to show you the ropes if you need a tutor." He winks before snagging another muffin and turning on his heels to head back to his cubicle, leaving me wondering if he meant show me the ropes of the site, or *show me the ropes*.

Surely it's the former, right? The teeny-bopper intern didn't just hit on me, right?

"Oh god," I groan, cradling my head in my hands. What have I gotten myself into? More to the point, what has *Susan* gotten me into?

Chapter five

I can't believe she talked me into this. I don't do blind dates as a rule, let alone blind dates with an internet stranger. Something about them just puts me on edge. I mean, he could be a serial killer, or worse, a politician! What would we even talk about?

"You look hot." Susan lounges across my bed with her third glass of wine. "I'd do you."

"Thanks, but you're not really my type." I poke my tongue out at her reflection in the mirror as I smooth my hands down the front of my dress once again. I'm still not happy with her about signing me up to that site, but I have to admit, it was a nice feeling to know someone chose me out of all the other options out there. Still, my nerves are all over the place. "Are you sure about this?"

"That you look hot? Hell yes."

I roll my eyes, turning to face her. "No, about this HookUp thing. Are you sure it's safe?"

She places her glass on the bedside table and sits up. "You're meeting in a public place, where lots of people will be. And if something doesn't feel right, send me a sneaky SOS text and I'll call you with some fake emergency." Pushing up off the bed, she stands in front of me with her hands on my shoulders. "I know I said you needed to get laid, but don't even think about that, okay? Just go out there and have a good time. I think you've earned it after Ernie, don't you?"

"He wasn't that bad," I whisper, averting my eyes.

"Don't do that. Don't make excuses for him. You're fucking gorgeous, and he's the idiot who couldn't see what was right in front of him."

I nod. It's not the first time she's given me this pep talk over the years. My self-esteem took a dive when I walked in on my husband sleeping with his receptionist. Talk about your cliché. She was young and perky, and I was, well, not. He said I'd let myself go and he wasn't attracted to me anymore. It was the most humiliating time of my life, even more so than the *Deep Heat* fiasco, and that's saying something.

"Let me just touch up my makeup." I walk into the bathroom and study my reflection. Since that day in Ernie's office, I vowed I would make more of an effort. I lost ten kilos, had my hair styled and coloured, and tried to keep up with the latest fashion trends. It could be exhausting sometimes, but if that's what it takes to be attractive, then so be it. Who cares that this is the first time in three years that all that effort is actually being put to use?

I reapply my lippy and take one final spin in front of the mirror before Susan drags me out of the bathroom. "Stop already. You're gonna be late."

Wringing my hands together, I say, "You promise you'll ring if I need you?"

"I promise. Just, give it a chance, okay? I know I've kinda thrown you in the deep end here, but you deserve to be happy." With her hands on my shoulders, she gives a gentle shove towards the door. "Now, go get 'em, tiger!" She slaps my arse as I walk through the door and down the stairs to grab my purse.

It's just one drink, I tell myself as I pull the door closed behind me. *I can do this.*

###

I so can *not* do this!

My breath comes in short, sharp pants as I lean against the car door, staring up at the crowded bar. I can't go in there. I just can't. I don't do things like this. I sit at home with a bottle of wine and my recipes, not go to bars to meet strange men. I'm perfectly happy staying at home by myself. Sure, it can get a little lonely at times, but maybe I could get a cat or three and become one of those crazy cat ladies. That has to be better than disappointing another man… I stop myself, shaking my head.

Jesus, where did that come from? That's Ernie talking if ever I heard it. I hate that he's made me doubt myself so much. I used to be a strong, confident woman, and now here I am, hyperventilating in a carpark over meeting someone new.

I close my eyes and take a deep breath. *They're not all like him.* The crinkle-eyed smile of Doctor Hottie flashes in my mind, and somehow that calms me down.

With renewed purpose, I push my shoulders back, lift my chin, and take that first step forward, only to find my dress is caught in the door. As I'm bent down, wrestling with the fabric, I hear my name being called. Jerking my head up a little too quickly, I lose my balance and fall backwards, my dress tearing as I smack my head into the side mirror. The wind is knocked out of me as I land with a thud on the ground, and the last thing I hear are footsteps pounding towards me.

Chapter six

A warm, musky scent mixed with disinfectant swirls around me as I come to. Blinking my eyes a few times to clear them, I'm greeted with stark white walls, and a full-size skeleton hanging out in the corner of the room. I'm getting a real sense of dejá vu here.

My head throbs as I move to sit up, and gentle hands guide me back down to the hard mattress beneath me. "Not too fast, Marianne. We can't have you blacking out again." I must be dreaming, because Doctor Hottie is right there, smiling down at me. "I'm sorry I startled you back there, it wasn't my intention."

A frown creases my brow as I realise this isn't a dream and somehow, I've found myself back in the hospital under the care of the hot doctor once again. I try to remember how I ended up in here, and suddenly it all comes flooding back. The bar, my dress caught in the door, and the voice calling my name. "That was you at the bar?" I stammer, pushing up onto my elbows.

He nods, offering a sheepish grin. "Guilty."

"*You* called my name?"

He rakes a hand through his hair with a chuckle. "Ah, yeah. I was trying to pluck up the courage to go inside the bar when I saw you struggling with your dress." He glances down at the torn fabric clinging to my thigh. "I didn't mean to startle you. It looked like you needed a hand."

"That's what got me into this mess in the first place," I groan.

"I'm sorry?"

What the hell, he's already been fishing inside the tunnel of love; no point in being embarrassed now. "After last week's... incident, my friend Susan discovered that it's been a while since I've had any action... down there." I tip my head towards my lady garden. "She said I needed to get back out there and set me up on a blind date with some guy on HookUp.com." I wince at how tragic it all sounds. "That's why I was at the bar. Well, in the carpark. I nearly didn't go in," I admit before my eyes widen and I slap a hand across my mouth. "Oh my God! My date! He'll think I stood him up!" Rolling to my side, I scan the room for my purse. "Have you seen my phone anywhere?"

He stands and retrieves my purse from the desk behind him. Before handing it to me, he cocks his head to the side with an odd expression on his face. "Out of interest, what was his name? The guy you were meeting tonight?"

"Dallas something, I think. Why?" Fumbling through the plethora of items in my purse that really don't need to be there, I make a promise to myself to sort through this mess when I get home. Of course, my phone is right at the bottom, buried under receipts and tissues. I pull it out to see no new messages or missed calls. Huh. Well if that doesn't feel like a kick in the teeth, I don't know what does.

"Ah…" He laughs. "You're not going to believe this, but I think *I'm* your date." He holds his hand out to me. "Dallas Mahoney."

Wait, what?

"*You're* my date?" I say in a falsetto tone. What are the chances?

"It would appear so."

"*I was trying to pluck up the courage to go inside…*"

"Wait, so you nearly didn't go inside? You were going to stand me up?" My voice cracks as reality sinks in. Doctor Hottie was going to bail on me. Every insecurity I felt that day in Ernie's office comes crashing back to me, and I wrap my arms around myself.

"Honestly? The thought crossed my mind."

I nod, wrapping my arms tighter as if they can hold me together. Ignoring the pounding in my head, I sit up, swing my legs over the edge of the bed and with a shaky hand, I grab my purse and clutch it to my body. "I'll save you the trouble." I storm towards the door with my head tucked into my chest, fighting back the tears that want to come. I will *not* let him see me cry over this.

"What? No, Marianne, that's not what I meant."

I pause with my hand on the door, not willing to face him. "It's okay." I turn my head to the side and offer him a weak smile, keeping my eyes averted. "Really, I understand. I'll let you get back to your night."

"Wait." His fingers curl around my wrist, stopping me. "Let me explain, please?"

His voice sounds pained and sincere, and it's for that reason I give him the benefit of the doubt and turn around slowly. Taking a breath, I steel myself for what he's about to say before meeting his gaze. "I'm listening."

His hand slips from my wrist to my hand, and he gently tugs, leading me back to the bed. I perch on the edge, ready to run if I need to.

Dallas sits beside me, his eyes closed as he takes a breath. "My wife died five years ago." *Definitely not what I was expecting him to say.* "I haven't been on a date since, but, like you, my best friend thought it was time too." He shrugs, staring at a space on the wall. "He set the whole thing up. I didn't even have a picture to go by, just a description. I had no idea it was you I was meeting. If I did—" he takes my hand, "—I never would've considered walking away." I search his eyes for signs of deceit but all I see is honesty. "I was scared, I guess. Five years is a long time to be out of the dating game, and I was worried I'd mess it all up." His gaze falls to our hands before flitting back to meet my gaze. "That's when I saw you, and something inside clicked. I realised I didn't want to be on a blind date with some random woman, I wanted to be on a date with you. That's why I called your name." He rakes a hand through his hair, a blush colouring his cheeks as he huffs out a nervous breath. "It's weird, isn't it?"

With a quirk of my brow, I purse my lips. "So, you saw me, the woman who pleasured herself with a tube of

Deep Heat and had to have it removed by you, no less, and thought, screw the lady I'm here to meet, she's the one for me?" I shake my head, half in disbelief and half amused. "I'm not sure what to make of that."

He winces. "I mean, it wasn't exactly the thought that went through my mind at the time, but yeah, I guess you could put it that way. Something inside you called to me." I snort, grinning, and he scrubs a hand down his face. "That's not what I meant. I didn't mean it like that." He chuckles. "I am really not coming across the way I was hoping to."

"Whatever gave you that impression?" I smirk, pushing up from the bed. "I have an idea. Do you want to maybe restart this night?" I hold my hand out to him. "Hi, I'm Marianne."

He takes it, his lips curling into a delicious grin that makes his eyes sparkle. "Hi, Marianne, I'm Dallas. And I'd like that very much."

Chapter seven

He leans back in his seat, taking a sip of his drink as he watches me. Never in all my life have I wanted to be an inanimate object so much as I want to be that glass right now. There's something deliciously appealing about this man. He's so comfortable in his own skin—not that I can blame him—the man's a dreamboat. He's got the whole George Clooney vibe going for him. And he's really rocking the silver hair.

Pulling a strand of my own coloured hair between my fingers, I can't help but wonder what it would look like if I let my natural colour grow out. Would there even be any colour to it at all? Would I rock grey hair as well as he does?

"So, why the fake name? I thought I was meeting Mary, not Marianne." His smirk is adorable, but it doesn't compare to when he brings out the big guns and makes his eyes crinkle.

"Oh, you know." I grin, waving a hand through the air. "I couldn't be giving my real name out to a serial killer." My eyes meet his as I toy with the tiny umbrella in my drink. It had actually been Susan's idea to change my name after I freaked out on her when I found out Daniel had seen my profile.

"Serial killer, eh? You have quite the imagination." He chuckles as he retrieves a pair of wire-rimmed glasses from his pocket.

"Considering how we first met, I think you already know that." I lean forward, nodding towards the spectacles he's wiping with a cloth. "You wear glasses?"

"I do." He nods, placing them on his face. I didn't think it was possible, but they make the blue of his eyes pop even more. "The old peepers aren't quite what they used to be, unfortunately." He shrugs. "It's all a part of getting older, and to be honest—" he leans in conspiratorially, "—I like to be able to see what I'm looking at. Especially something as beautiful as you."

I raise my brows. "Wow. That was…"

"Cheesy?"

I grin, holding my finger and thumb in the air. "Little bit."

He throws his head back as he laughs. "This is why I like you; you're funny, and honest to a fault."

Am I though? Here I am, my face plastered in makeup, my hair coloured to within an inch of its life, and too afraid to wear my prescription glasses for fear they'll make me look old. Perhaps I should take a leaf out of his book.

"You want honest? This isn't my natural hair colour. Well, it is, but chemicals help keep it that way." I cover my face with my hands. "In fact, I haven't seen my natural colour in three years. It could be green for all I know." I peek through my fingers to see he's not looking at me with disgust. Dropping my hands, I rummage through my purse and pull out my glasses case. "I'm meant to wear glasses too, but I'm too vain to do so." I plonk them on the table between us, breathing a sigh of relief at finally coming clean. The only times they make it out of my purse is in the comfort of my own home, and only because I can't make out the sudoku puzzles without them, and my eyes are so tired by the end of the day from having to strain at the computer screen all day long.

Dallas takes my hands in his. "You know, beauty is more than skin deep. Who cares if you have green hair or wear glasses? It's what's inside that matters, and I think there's something special inside you, Marianne."

"No." I shake my head. "You removed that, remember?" I quirk a brow at him, and he laughs. A loud, raucous laugh that turns a few heads, but he doesn't even care.

"I'm going to have my hands full with you."

I look down at my chest, squeezing my arms in tight to push my boobs together. "I mean, they're a little more than a handful, I would've thought. And that's very presumptuous of you, doc." I grin, plucking the strawberry from my drink and placing it in my mouth. "You haven't even bought me dinner yet."

His cheeks flush again, and he shakes his head with a chuckle. "Where are my manners?" He hands me a menu but doesn't let go straight away. Nodding towards my glasses, he whispers, "Put them on," and somehow it sounds ridiculously sexy.

"Um." I pull my lip between my teeth as I meet his gaze.

"Please?"

"Okay," I say quietly. Flipping the case open, I pull the white frames out and place them on my face with a flourish. "Tada."

He sucks in a breath, his lips slowly curling into an appreciative grin. "You are stunning."

And in this moment, with him looking at me like that, I *feel* stunning. It's an odd sensation that sends heat thrumming through my veins.

I can't recall a time when Ernie *ever* made me feel this way; like I was beautiful without even trying. Even in our early days he was scarce on the compliments. I suppose that should have been a warning sign right there. I never really had a hope in hell. It was inevitable that I would be replaced with a younger, perkier version of myself, I just didn't want to admit that my husband of so many years could be so shallow.

I've spent these last three years primping and priming myself in some weird form of retaliation to show my ex-husband I'm not the washed-up old woman he made me out to be. The funny thing is, we don't even roll in the same circles anymore. I go out of my way to avoid all the old haunts, so I don't have to witness him canoodling with the secretary or whoever his latest conquest is.

It really is a sad state of existence I've been holding myself in. What's worse, is that I don't even know why. I may still have hang-ups over our relationship and how he made me feel, but I'm in no way pining for the man anymore. That ship well and truly sailed once I saw his naked arse ploughing into that blonde bimbo of his. There's something very unappealing about seeing your forty-year-old husband with his pants around his ankles and his socks pulled up to his knees, pounding away at a very flexible twenty-year old. It's a mental image I could've done without, and one that haunted my dreams for a good twelve months after the fact.

Still, it doesn't explain why I've chosen to live the life of a nun, albeit looking damn good while doing so.

Offering Dallas a smile, I tip my head to the side. "Well, if I'm going to get that kind of reaction when I wear them, I might just have to start wearing them every day."

"You should. They suit you." He reaches out, brushing a strand of hair behind my ear, and just that simple touch sends a tingle coursing through my body and making itself at home between my thighs. One lingering touch is all it takes to have me practically melting into a puddle. What kind of weird hot-doctor voodoo is this?

He chuckles, and I realise I'm staring at him like a lovesick puppy. Nodding to the menu, he asks, "Do you know what you want?"

Yes, you.

My cheeks burn as those words dance around in my head, but I clear my throat and turn my eyes back to the menu, only just noticing the waitress who appeared out of nowhere beside me. God, how long was I staring at him? "Uh, I'm not sure. Everything sounds so good." I wave him on. "You order first."

"Okay, I'll just have the beef burger with a side of fries and aioli please." He smiles as he hands back the menu, and I can see how smitten the waitress is when those crinkles around his eyes come out. She does a sort of half-curtsey while biting her lip and twirling her finger in her hair.

"Uh, hi." I wave to get her attention, and she huffs out a sigh, turning to me with a quirk of her brow. "I'll have what he's having." I hand the menu back with a sickly-sweet smile, reaching out to grasp Dallas's hand. She huffs again, then turns on her heels, making her way out to the kitchen, no doubt to spit in my food.

When I turn back to Dallas, he's watching me with amusement, and I drop my head into my hand with a snort. I peek between my fingers. "Was that too much?"

He chuckles, threading his fingers through mine. "Not at all. It was actually kind of sexy."

"It was?"

"Oh yeah." He leans in. "But if I'm honest, it's no competition." He hooks a thumb over his shoulder towards the kitchen with a shake of his head. "She's not my type."

My brows practically hit the ceiling as I pull back, folding my arms across my chest. "Young, attractive, and fawning over you isn't your type?"

He settles back in his seat, lifting his drink to his lips slowly. "Nope. I prefer my women like I prefer my wine; mature and full-bodied."

I damn near spit my drink across the table. "Wow." I shake my head with a giggle. "You're on a roll tonight, doc." He tips his head with a wink. "Pretty proud of yourself for that one, aren't you?"

Clasping his hands on the table, he leans forward. "Come on, you have to admit, that was clever."

"It was something, that's for sure."

"As long as it keeps you here with me, I'll take it." Heat blooms in my chest. How does he make me feel so much with just a softly spoken word or the touch of a finger? It's as though I've lived my life with my head in the sand and I'm only now discovering the good stuff. For the first time since it happened, I'm glad I wound up with my legs in stirrups and Dallas by my side.

Chapter eight

Waking up with a grin on my face is something new, but it feels good. It feels *really* good. Last night ended up being so much better than I could've anticipated, and we didn't even have sex! Dallas is old school; preferring to wine and dine and actually date before moving to the next level, and I am more than okay with that. It's nice to be courted for once. Certainly makes a change from Ernie and his wandering hands from day one. Yet another sign I neglected to pay attention to. Oh well, you live and learn.

We spent hours chatting at the restaurant, and no matter how many times the waitress batted her eyes at Dallas, he never turned his attention from me. It made me feel wanted, special, like I was being put first. If it wasn't for his taking it slow and getting to know each other idea, I would've been all over him like a rash. There's something about a man who knows what or who he wants and isn't afraid to show it, that really gets my motor running.

The things I would do to that man…

I bite my lip as that familiar heat surges through my body, pooling in the apex of my thighs. If only he'd taken me up on the offer of a night cap. The skilled hands of a doctor could certainly be put to use right about now. I bet he can do things I haven't even thought of.

My phone pings beside me, and I consider ignoring it so I can continue with my fantasy, but the only person who would be texting me at this time of the morning on a Saturday is Susan, and I know she won't let up until I respond with a full-blown breakdown of what happened last night.

Snatching it up, I see two messages already on the screen: one in all caps.

Susan: I need details asap!

Susan: DON'T MAKE ME COME OVER THERE!

I giggle at her theatrics when the three dots start dancing across the screen.

Susan: Scratch that. I'm already on my way. Get your arse out of bed and put the jug on!

Rolling my eyes, I push the sheets back and swing my legs to the ground. So much for my leisurely lie in. I have approximately ten minutes before she'll be downstairs, pounding on my door. I should probably have a shower and make myself presentable, but ten minutes is barely long enough for the water to heat in the shower, let alone do my hair and put my face on. And if I learned anything from Dallas last night, it's that I don't need to put so much pressure on myself to "look presentable". I'm stunning just the way I am, morning breath and all.

Well, maybe not the morning breath part. I can at least get my teeth brushed before she arrives and wants a blow by blow.

Instead of scrutinising my appearance in the mirror as I would normally do, I take a moment to appreciate the things that make me, me. My unruly curls have always been the bane of my existence, but today I notice the way they frame my face just so. My blue eyes aren't as vibrant as they used to be, but they're still my best feature, and even the tiny lines forming around the edges don't bother me this morning; it means I've smiled a lot over the years.

Screw what Ernie said. I haven't let myself go. I've covered up the *real* me, and for what? To prove something to my shallow ex-husband? I can't believe I wasted so much time and effort on someone who clearly couldn't care less about me. Well, no more! Today is a new day, and today I embrace this whole growing-old-gracefully thing.

With a bounce in my step, I make my way to the kitchen with a new sudoku puzzle in hand, ready to get started on breakfast and wait for Susan.

Pancake batter is made, and the jug has barely clicked off before she's hammering on the door. "Open up, Coochie Mama!" I pour a dollop of batter into the pan before rushing to the door.

"Isn't it Hoochie Mama?" I ask as I usher her inside before the neighbours complain.

She waves my comment off, dumping her bag on the chair in the hall. "Nope. You're a coochie mama, ya know, because you got," she gestures towards my nether regions, "*Deep Heat* all up in your coochie." She waggles her eyebrows, and I can't help but laugh as I flip the pancake over and grab a plate.

"I'm never going to live that down, am I?"

"Nope. Not so long as I am here to remind you." She grins, helping herself to a fork and digging into my breakfast. With her mouth full of food, she grabs a mug, adding three heaped teaspoons of coffee and another four of sugar.

"Rough night?" I ask, nodding my head to her syrupy drink.

She rolls her eyes then takes a large gulp of her drink. "I wish. What I wouldn't give for a bit of rough and tumble between the sheets right about now. I don't know how you've gone three years without. This dry spell, and I mean *dry,* is killing me!" She puts her cup down and braces her elbows on the counter, leaning forward. "Please tell me you had better luck? I didn't get any SOS message, so that's gotta be good, right?" She takes another bite of my pancake, licking the maple syrup from her lips.

I try to play it coy but fail as a grin slips across my face. I bring the cup to my lips and give a small nod. "It was nice."

"Nice? Just nice? Jesus, Mary and Joseph, give me something more than that! What was he like? Are you seeing him again? Did you get bizzay?" She thrusts her pelvis and rolls her hips, which sets me off laughing.

"Bizzay? Who are you? Beyoncé or something?"

"It's Susancé, thank you very much. And don't change the subject. Did you not hear I'm having a dry spell? Let me live vicariously through you, like a good friend." Resting her chin on her hands, she flutters her eyelashes at me, all doe-eyed.

"There's not much to tell." I shrug, taking another slow drink of my coffee and peering over the rim at her. "Except that Dallas Mahoney is none other than Doctor Hottie."

"Get out of town! *The* Doctor Hottie? The one who fished things out of your vajayjay?"

"The one and the same." I think back to the way he looked at me throughout the evening, and I can't help but smile. "He told me I was stunning."

Her eyes soften and she takes my hand. "That's because you *are* stunning. I've been telling you that for years."

"I know, it's just—"

"It's different when it comes from a man. Especially a dreamboat of a man who happens to be a doctor." She waggles her brows again. "Is he a good kisser? I bet he is. Real attentive." She sighs, getting a faraway look in her eyes.

"I don't know. He didn't kiss me. Well, not on the lips."

"Oh, I hear what you're saying." She nods, holding her hand up for a high five. "Got yourself a little tongue-lashing downstairs. Mmmmhmm."

"Get your mind out of the gutter, *Susancé*. There was none of that going on. He was a gentleman." I smooth my hands down the front of my robe, letting them rest on my lap.

Susan's lips scrunch up as she rears her head back. "Ugh, a gentleman. Who wants one of those?"

Shaking my head, I gather our empty mugs and take them to the sink. "You're incorrigible. I happen to like it. He's sweet and charming." She makes a gagging sound and mimes sticking her finger down her throat, so I flick her with the dishcloth. "He makes me laugh, and I feel good when I'm with him." I turn back to the sink. "Sex isn't everything, you know. We're making a connection first."

"You know what else can make a connection? His junk and your coochie." She nods, folding her arms across her chest. "That's the kind of connection I'm interested in."

"Well you're gonna have to wait for a while then, because we're taking things slow." I dry my hands then fold the towel into a neat square.

"You're a stronger woman than I. Three years between sexcapades and I'd be climbing the man like Jack and that beanstalk of his." She pulls her bottom lip between her teeth. "I'd climb him so damn hard."

"Of course you would, Miss One-and-Done. I wouldn't expect *you* to understand the benefits of waiting." I quirk a brow, challenging her to deny it.

"Pfft, please. This coming from the woman who ended up in the emergency room after defiling herself." She shakes her head. "You're telling me if Mr. Hotness himself told you it was on like Donkey Kong, you wouldn't jump his bones?" She places her hands on her hips, pursing her lips.

I could deny it, but we both know I'd be lying. Yes, I've been celibate the last three years, but that doesn't mean I wouldn't jump at the chance to have a roll in the hay if it was on offer. I mean, I'm only human, and the man is gorgeous.

"I'm going to take your silence as an admission. You want to let the doc probe you with his stethoscope." She says it in a dirty sing-song way, rolling her hips and pulling a weird face. God, I hope that's not her sex face.

Covering my mouth, I stifle a giggle. "That is so wrong on so many levels. Firstly, I don't think he's the kind of doctor to 'probe' people, and I'm pretty sure that's not what a stethoscope is for." I tilt my head, trying to picture what that would look like. "How would that even work? Which part goes in first? The round bit or the earpiece?" My eyes widen as that conjures up a ghastly image. I shake my head. "Nope. I don't think it's possible."

"Who cares how it works? The point is, you'd let him try if he asked nicely." She waggles her eyebrows, and I roll my eyes with a sigh.

"All right, fine. Yes, if he wanted to 'probe' me, I wouldn't say no. There. Happy now?"

"I am. Very." Draping her upper body across the counter and resting her head on her arm, she looks up at me with a goofy grin. "So, when are you seeing him next?"

Chapter nine

"Morning, Marianne. What have you got for us today?" Daniel asks as I enter the office. I've been bringing my weekend baking in every Monday for the past year, and he's always the first to dive in.

I hold up the plate. "White chocolate brownies."

"Noice!" He snaffles the largest corner piece and takes a bite. His eyes roll back as he tilts his head and says, "Damn that's good." Leaning his hip against my desk, he devours the whole piece in thirty seconds flat. "Seriously, Marianne, you are wasting your talent here. You should be on *Masterchef* or something. Or at the very least, you should be selling this stuff. It's dynamite!"

"Well, thank you, but I don't think anyone wants to see this face on TV, or buy my home baking."

He frowns, shaking his head. "I'm not even going near that first comment, but you seriously underestimate your skills." He grabs another brownie from the plate. "These are your best yet. I would happily pay you to make me a batch of these every week. Seriously. You should think about it."

I nod to placate him, but it's just a dream from my past life. I couldn't make a living out of this. "Thanks, I will."

"How was your weekend anyway?" He's normally full of stories from his weekend, as young people are, and I very rarely have anything to share that would be of any interest to him. It's really just a courtesy he offers me, and I doubt he'd be fascinated by my wine-drinking escapades with Susan, but today I feel like sharing.

"Actually, pretty good." I glance side to side then lean towards him with a grin. "I had a date. You know, from the, um," I drop my voice even lower, "site."

His eyes widen before a smile splits his face. "Yeah, girl, get you some." He pulls a face and thrusts his hips back and forth, but instead of being mortified as I would normally be, I can't help but grin back at him. Being with Dallas, even for only one night, has given me a new lease on life.

"I don't know that I 'got me some', but I think we're going to see each other again."

"Wait. You *think*?" He stops his thrusting and raises a brow.

"Well, yeah. He's a doctor and he was on call most of the weekend, so we couldn't see each other again." His face drops, and I instantly feel anxious. "Is that bad?"

"I don't know, Marianne." He purses his lips, leaning his hip against my desk. "I mean, I've used the old 'I'm a doctor' line to get a chick before, but only because it was a one-time thing, ya know?" He looks at me with pity. "Sorry."

"Oh, no, he really is a doctor. I actually met him when I was in the hospital the other week."

"You were in the hospital?" His eyes bug out. "You okay?"

I wave a hand through the air dismissively. "Oh yeah, I'm fine." I clear my throat. "It was nothing."

"Cool, cool." He nods. "Look, the way I see it, if I'm into a girl, I let her know it's on, ya know? Like nothing would stop me from seeing her… even work."

"Oh." I let my head drop, and I busy myself with restacking the papers on my desk. This morning just took a nosedive. "So, you think he fobbed me off then?"

"I don't know. Maybe?" It must show on my face how disappointed I am because he quickly follows up with, "It's probably just me, though. I'm no doctor." He shrugs then reaches out and awkwardly pats my arm. "I'm sure he's into you. What's not to like? You're pretty hot for an—" He stops, clearing his throat and shuffling his feet. "You're pretty hot."

I nod, offering a small smile in thanks. It's sweet he's trying to make me feel better, even if in a backhanded kind of way. "I hope so. He seemed like he was genuine." I glance around the room again, then lower my voice. "We didn't, um, you know…"

"Seal the deal?"

"Yeah. He said he wanted to take things slow. But maybe that's the reason?" There's hope in my voice, and I suddenly feel like I'm a teenager again. I mean, I'm turning to the *intern* for dating advice. This is a new low for me.

Daniel grins. "Shoot, why didn't you say so? If a guy says he wants to see you again, and you haven't done the nasty already, then he's legit into you."

"Really?"

"Oh for sure. If he only wanted a shag, he'd have got it done that first night. Too much effort to play the long game." He backs towards the adjoining door to his office. "You might have found yourself one of the only guys on HookUp.com who isn't just after a bit of slap and tickle."

###

At morning teatime, I pour myself a coffee and settle back at my desk. I rifle through my bag for my phone and am pleasantly surprised by the message awaiting me.

Dallas: I woke up thinking of you. I had a really nice time on Friday, and I'm hoping you'll let me take you out again this weekend? I'm not on call, so I can be yours all weekend, if you'll have me.

I reread his message with what I'm sure is a goofy grin plastered on my face. He wants to see me again, and for the whole weekend, no less.

Marianne: I had a lovely time too; and having you all weekend sounds fabulous.

I hit send, then realise what I just said. I didn't mean *having* him having him, but how do I say that without sounding like I don't want him? Because I do. I want him more than I've wanted anything in my life. And not just because he's gorgeous, but because he makes me feel good about myself, and it's been a long time since I've felt that.

Before I can think of how to rephrase my message, the tell-tale sound of a message being written pipes up from my phone. My cheeks flush as I watch the three dots jump on the screen then disappear. They do that three times before a reply comes through, and by this time I'm about ready to march into Daniel's office and ask for his help. I'm so out of my depth here.

Turns out, I don't have anything to worry about.

Dallas: You can have me any way you'd like.

Chapter ten

The rest of the week is uneventful as we're both busy with work, but sure enough, come Friday afternoon, I get those tingles of anticipation running through my body. It makes me feel like I'm back in high school and Dallas is the star first five. Not that I was ever really into sports or sportsmen; though those tiny shorts and skin-tight jerseys are pretty nice to look at. Especially when they're doing lunges down the field to warm up. Now *that* is something I could watch all day.

I let out a dreamy sigh as I rest my chin on the palm of my hand, staring sightlessly at the screen in front of me. All thoughts of work have up and flown away, and all I can think about is Dallas in a pair of rugby shorts. I bet he'd rock them like he rocks everything else. In fact, I wouldn't be surprised if he played. He does have those broad shoulders and strong thighs. I tug my bottom lip between my teeth as I envisage him lunging down the field with those muscular thighs of his.

"Right, I'm out," Daniel says from beside me, jolting me from my thoughts. I quickly wipe the drool from my lips before I turn to him. He's grinning from ear to ear. "Good luck with the doc. Have a *good* weekend,

Marianne." He waggles his eyebrows at me as if he knows what I was thinking about. "Don't do anything I wouldn't do."

"I feel like there's not much on the list of things you wouldn't do."

He belts out a laugh, shaking his head. "True story."

"Have a good weekend, Daniel."

He brings two fingers to his forehead in a sort of salute as he walks out the door, hollering, "You too."

As soon as he's gone, I quickly shut down the computer that's been on the same screen for the last half an hour, sign out, gather my things, and rush out the door to get ready for my date with Dallas.

"Knock, knock," Susan calls as she lets herself in. "Door was open."

I run down the stairs, my shoes in hand and face half done. "What are you doing here?"

She flings her bag on the counter, placing her hands on her hips. "Nice to see you too."

"You know what I mean. Dallas will be here any second."

"Oh, that was tonight? Oops, silly me." She flutters her eyes in an attempt to look innocent, but I'm not buying it. Not for a second.

Narrowing my eyes, I point a finger at her chest. "Don't play coy with me. I know what you're up to."

"Why, whatever do you mean?" She places a hand to her chest, but her eyes give her away.

"You're such a perv."

"Oh, come on, I just want a peek at Doctor Hottie. See if he's as hot as you said." She presses her tongue to the inside of her cheek. "I just wanna see who has my friend so smitten. Is that so wrong?"

"Smitten?" a deep voice pipes up from the doorway. Susan and I turn to each other with wide eyes, and I give her a pleading look, which she promptly ignores.

Spinning on her heels, she flings her hand out towards Dallas. "You must be Doctor Hot—" I elbow her before she can finish.

"Doctor Hot?" He turns to me with a look of amusement, and as much as I'd like the floor to open and swallow me up right now, I find myself grinning back at him. It's impossible not to when he's looking at me like that.

I offer him my hand. "Hi, I'm Marianne, and I objectify men. Sorry." I shrug because what else can I do at this point?

"And I'm Susan, the best friend who also objectifies men, but I'm not sorry about it." She steps in front of me, taking his hand and, no doubt, giving him the once over. She peeks back at me over her shoulder, mouthing the words, *oh my god.*

"And she was just leaving, weren't you, Suz?"

"I was? Oh," she clears her throat, "I was." She nods, gathering her bag from the counter. She wraps her arms around me, whispering, "I totally agree with you.

He's hot with a capital H," under her breath before backing towards the door.

Dallas skirts out of her way, but not before she levels him with a glare. "You hurt her, I hurt you, capeesh?"

"Oh my god, bye, Susan." I give her a gentle shove to get her moving, but she holds his gaze, bringing two fingers up in the universal sign of 'I'm watching you'.

He places a hand to his chest and does a sort of bow. "My intentions with Marianne are pure, I assure you."

That stops her in her tracks. "Well, not too pure, I hope." She waggles her eyebrows, waving a hand through the air in my direction. "She's been out of action for a loooooooong time, if you get my drift."

Could she be any more embarrassing?

"Susan, please leave, now." I give her another shove towards the door as I speak through gritted teeth.

"Okay, okay. I know when I'm not wanted. Geez." She holds her hands up in surrender then slings her bag over her shoulder. With a final wave, she brings her hand to her ear with her finger and thumb extended. "Call me later."

"Will do."

"It really was nice to meet you, Dallas."

"You too."

I follow her to the door to make sure she actually leaves, then head back through to the kitchen. "Sorry about her."

He chuckles. "She seems fun."

"She has her moments." I perch on the stool and slip my feet into my heels. "Let me just finish up my make-up, then we're good to go."

With a finger under my chin, he lifts my face to meet his puzzled gaze. "Don't feel you need to on my account. You look perfect just the way you are."

My insides turn to mush, and I practically melt in his hands. I know I was full of bravado after our last date, deciding to show the real me, but then reality hit as soon as I stepped out my front door into the real world. It's one thing to reveal my bare face to Susan, it's a whole other thing to reveal it to the world. I couldn't do it. But now, with him looking at me this way? Maybe I can be brave enough. "I, um, okay. Really? Because I was only half done." I try to turn my head to catch a glimpse of myself in the mirror by the door, but he holds me still.

"Really. You don't need it."

I'm sure my face has turned all shades of pink as I let his words settle over me. I never used to wear make-up, not until Ernie made me feel I wasn't up to par. Now it's more of a habit than anything else. A mask I wear to protect myself. I don't think I've left the house without a full face on in years, but I have to admit, the idea of going out fresh-faced, with Dallas by my side, is somewhat appealing. Freeing even.

Before I can have a panic attack and change my mind, I grab my bag and follow him out the door.

Chapter eleven

We pull up to a quaint little coffee shop tucked away between two large department stores. It's the kind of place you could easily overlook during the day if you didn't know it was there, but with the sun setting behind it, the twinkling fairy lights that adorn the window give it an almost ethereal glow.

"How did you find this place?" I ask as we step through the threshold into a warmth that can only be achieved with a log fire. Worn leather couches of different colours sit around the central fireplace, and surrounding those are smaller tables and chairs, offering a little more privacy.

Taking my coat and hanging it on the rack by the door, Dallas places his hand to the small of my back and leads me to one of the couches. "One of my colleagues recommended it. They make a great hot chocolate, and their desserts are divine."

"Straight to dessert? A man after my own heart."

"That's the plan," he says so quietly I nearly miss it.

We settle in, our legs turned towards each other, and a waitress comes around with a menu and two glasses of water.

"Hi, guys, can I get you anything to drink?"

"If I may," Dallas says, one brow rising as he looks to me.

"Go ahead. I trust you."

His eyes light up as he smiles then turns his attention back to the waitress. "Two of your decadent hot chocolates please."

The waitress nods, then leaves us to ourselves. Dallas pulls out his glasses and leans back as he peruses the menu. He brings his arm to rest on the back of the couch, and his fingers gently brush against my neck, sending a shiver through me.

"They use melted Belgian chocolate to make the drinks. They're one of the best things you can put in your mouth." His eyes flick up to mine briefly, and there's a hint of colour in his cheeks as he chuckles. "You know what I mean."

I would normally come up with something crass to say about now, but all I can think about is the way his fingers feel against my skin. So soft and gentle, like a sweet caress. It seems like a lifetime ago that anyone touched me like this. I'd forgotten how good it feels. And to think, I've deprived myself of this for the past three years. All because of a two-faced jerk.

Dallas's fingers move to smooth the skin of my brow, and I realise I must've been frowning over my thoughts. "What is it?" he asks.

Way to ruin a moment, Marianne.

I shake my head. "Doesn't matter. It's not important." I plaster a smile on my face to prove it.

He purses his lips but doesn't say a word, and somehow that makes me want to open up to him. It must be some of that doctor voodoo they all seem to have.

"I was just thinking how long it's been since anyone has touched me like this." I gesture to the hand kneading my neck and shoulder. "It feels so much better than I remember." I glance at him out the corner of my eye. "Must be those magic doctor fingers of yours."

He chuckles. "Magic, eh?"

"That's what they say. But maybe that needs to be tested. I am more than prepared to volunteer as a test subject." He increases the pressure at the base of my neck, and I can't help but moan and lean my head forward.

"Here." He takes hold of my shoulder and gently pulls me to face away from him, and his expert fingers begin kneading both my shoulders. It's so good I have to consciously stop myself from purring.

"Mmhmm, definitely magic." The thought of those same hands touching me in other places sends a jolt of pleasure through me, and I have to squeeze my thighs together for relief.

His breath tickles my ear as he leans in and whispers, "You keep making those noises and we might get kicked out."

I wave a hand through the air. "Worth it."

A rumble vibrates through my chest as he chuckles, pulling me against him. I nestle into the crook of his arm, and his hand falls to my hip as if it's second nature. He smooths my hair and rests his chin against the side of my head.

The waitress brings us our drinks, and Dallas orders an apple crumble with caramel sauce and a fudge brownie for us to share. We sit in a comfortable silence, watching the flames flicker in the fireplace as we wait for our drinks to cool.

"Can I ask you something, Marianne? You don't have to answer if you don't want to."

I'm so content in his arms, he could ask me just about anything and I would answer. "Fire away."

"I was just wondering how someone like you is still single. Not that I'm complaining. I'm just surprised you haven't been snatched up by anyone."

"Are you kidding me right now?" I roll my eyes and shake my head. "Look who's talking. I could say the same thing about you. You're quite the catch, Doctor Mahoney. I bet you're fending the girls off left, right, and centre."

He chuckles. "I'm flattered you think so, but I assure you, that's not the case."

"I think you underestimate the power of your silver fox status."

"You think I'm a silver fox?"

I lean back, my eyebrows nearly firing clean off my face. Surely he knows how attractive he is. "Um, yeah. Have you seen you?" I wave my hand down the length of his body.

"Every morning in the mirror." He grins. "But I believe you're changing the subject."

"Noticed that, did you?" I nestle back into the warmth of his chest.

"I did, and that's okay. I said you didn't have to answer. I was just curious. We can talk about something else."

I inhale a deep breath then huff it out. "No, it's fine. There's not much to tell really." I bring my hand up to rest on his chest, my fingers toying with the button closest. "I was married, before. And I didn't really realise what kind of relationship it was until it was too late." The arm Dallas has wrapped around me flexes, and his fingers curl into my hip protectively. I draw my knees up onto the couch, letting him hold me. "My ex-husband spent years breaking me down. He made me feel like I wasn't good enough, and I guess I believed him." I shrug as if it's not a big deal, when I know it is. I let his opinion of me cloud my own opinion of myself for far too long. Still do sometimes, if I'm honest.

I feel Dallas tense beside me, but I wave it off. "It is what it is. I'm starting to see that maybe he wasn't right."

A low growl rumbles through him, and he tilts my head up to face him. "There's no maybe about it. You are so much *more* than enough, Marianne." His lips brush against mine ever so gently, and he hovers there, our breaths mingling as he presses his forehead to mine. "He's a fool if he couldn't see that."

My breath catches in my throat as I close my eyes and press my lips to his once more. This man is challenging everything I have believed to be true for the past few wasted years of my life. I feel like I've been blinded and only now am I beginning to see things as they are. It makes me sad to think of all the things I've missed out on.

A throat clears as the waitress places our desserts on the table in front of us then backs away, leaving us in peace. We pull apart slowly, both of us grinning as we shuffle forward and tuck into our desserts.

I have to admit, he wasn't wrong when he said the hot chocolate and desserts were some of the best things you could have in your mouth. They are divine, and I've taken mental notes to try my own variations at some point. Right now, though, I can think of other things I'd rather be doing with my mouth, especially now that I've had a taste of him.

I'm all too aware of his thigh pressed against mine and the heat that radiates off him. I want to curl into his lap and stay there all night, but I know that's not where this is headed, not yet. Damn him and his gentlemanly virtue.

With the last of the desserts eaten, Dallas leans back on the couch, turning to me with a thoughtful expression. He stretches his arm across the back of the couch once more, and I don't need any more encouragement than that to snuggle into his side. There's something so comforting about being wrapped in his arms.

"Will you let me take you somewhere tomorrow?" he asks, his fingers trailing back and forth down my arm. "It's somewhere special to me, and I think you'll like it."

He can take me wherever he wants so long as he keeps touching me. I'm like putty in his hands. "You can take me anywhere you like. We have the whole weekend, right?"

He presses his lips to the top of my head. "That we do."

Chapter twelve

"When you said dress casual, I thought you meant jeans and a t-shirt, not whatever that is." I flick my finger in a circle, gesturing towards Dallas's oversized dungarees and frizzy green hair. "Are we running away to join the circus?"

He grins, and his eyes shine as he places a spongy red ball on the tip of his nose. "Close, but not quite." He offers his elbow with a tilt of his head. "Shall we?"

He's so adorable, in a goofy kind of way. I don't even care what he has planned, I'm in. "Lead the way."

"Did you remember your glasses?"

I pat my purse. "Of course, though I'm not sure what I'm going to need them for." I glance at him out the corner of my eye, still none the wiser as to what this date could entail. He doesn't strike me as one of those weird cult members who dress up like carnival folk to get their jollies off, but it wouldn't be the first time I'd got the wrong impression of someone. "It's not like I can lose you in a crowd dressed like that."

He holds his arm out to the side. "What? Is it too much?"

"Well, that all depends on what we're doing, doesn't it?" I rake my eyes from his toes to the tip of his head. "If we're going to a fair, then I'd say you're about perfect." I pause, pursing my lips. "If we're going to a restaurant though, I think you might be a tad overdressed."

He quirks a brow, pointing a finger at his chest. "Me? Overdressed?" He touches a hand to his gaudy wig. "It's the hair, isn't it?"

I press my lips together but can't contain the laughter that wants to bubble free. "Mmhmm, definitely the hair." Running a hand through my own unruly curls, I pout. "Will I fit in with this? Or do you have another one of those for me to wear?"

"I wouldn't dream of covering that up. You're perfect just the way you are." As seems to be happening more and more frequently these days, I find myself grinning like the cat who got the cream. A girl could get used to all these compliments.

When he pulls up outside the children's hospital, the clown get-up starts to make sense. Being a doctor is a selfless occupation in itself, add in donating his free time to entertain sick children, and the man is as close as one can get to being a saint. I swear I can feel my ovaries exploding as I'm filled with awe for this man and everything he does.

He turns the car off and rests his hands on his lap as if he's having second thoughts about bringing me here. Reaching out, I place my hand over his until he looks at me.

"I wasn't completely honest with you last weekend. I wasn't on call on Saturday, I was here, volunteering," he offers, swallowing audibly. "After what you told me last night, I wanted to share this with you. But now that we're here, I realise I probably should've asked you first. Sorry. I know hospitals can be triggers for some people. I wasn't thinking."

"Hey." I let my thumb trace circles across the back of his hand. "Stop freaking out. I think it's sweet that you volunteer, and very noble. I'm not sure what I can do, but I'd love to help out if I can. And if it means I get to see you act the clown, I'm all for it." I grin, giving his hand a squeeze.

His whole face lights up, and he chuckles. "Well that's great, I think." He rolls his eyes, then turns to me with a serious look. "I've been coming here every Saturday for a long time, but I've never brought anyone here before," he admits.

"Never? Not even your wife?"

He takes a deep breath, shaking his head, and I instantly regret saying anything. The look on his face is one of anguish, and I'd do anything to take back my stupid question. We barely broached the subject of our past marriages on our other dates, merely skimming over the details, and now I've gone and opened up an old wound.

"No, not even my wife." He stares across the parking lot at the doors to the hospital. "She ah, she died during childbirth. There were complications we didn't foresee, and…" He scrubs his hand across the rough stubble on his chin. "Neither of them made it." He turns to me with a sad smile. "That's when I started volunteering here. I needed to do something to make sense of it all, give it meaning, if that makes sense. I was a broken man, and these kids, they put me back together."

Tears pool in my eyes for the hurt he's endured. It's so unfair that anyone should have to go through that, let alone someone as altruistic as him. "Oh, Dallas, I'm so sorry. I had no idea."

He shakes his head again. "You weren't to know. It's not something I talk about. I probably should've explained before bringing you here." He shrugs, then turning his gaze back out the window, he says, "Offering my time is nothing compared to what some of these families go through. It's very humbling. Children see things in ways most adults choose not to." He flips his hand up to link our fingers together, bringing my hand to his lips. "They put things in perspective, and you learn not to take things for granted." He doesn't say it, but the look in his eyes makes me think he's talking about us, and I get a fluttering deep in my belly. He's too good for me. Too good for anyone. I turn my face from him to hide the tears still threatening to fall.

How can I possibly compare to the woman who died trying to bring their child into the world?

Brushing a wayward strand of hair from my face, he tilts my chin up until I meet his gaze. "Hey."

"Hey."

His thumb trails gently beneath my eye as a frown creases his forehead. "I know I've been out of the dating game a while, but I'm pretty sure you're not meant to cry on our third date." He grimaces. "I didn't mean to upset you or sound presumptuous. I only meant that I like you, and I don't take you for granted. And I want you to see yourself through their eyes."

I blink slowly. Here is this man, wearing his heart on his sleeve, sharing with me his own personal agony, and yet, he's checking on me, making sure I'm okay. What did I do to deserve a man like this?

I swivel around in my seat, taking his hands in mine. "I like you too, and I don't take you for granted either." With a small smile, I tap the red ball on his nose. "Even if it's hard to take you seriously when you're dressed like that."

He blinks, looking down at his brightly coloured dungarees and back up with a wide grin. "I suppose it's not my most debonair of outfits."

"It's not, no." I giggle. "But it might just be my favourite."

"Duly noted."

Inhaling deeply, I grab the door handle and nod my head towards the hospital. "Shall we go in then?"

Chapter thirteen

The change in Dallas when he steps through the doors to the children's ward is uncanny. I knew he had a sense of humour, but I never expected to be watching him dance around, telling jokes and singing silly songs to make the children laugh. And the way they stare up at him with their wide eyes so full of adoration is enough to melt the heart of even the iciest of souls.

"He's something else, isn't he?" one of the nurses standing behind me says. "He's here every Saturday, without fail, and he never seems to tire of it." She scribbles something on a clipboard then tucks it under her arm. "The children adore him."

I smile, watching him juggle balls unsuccessfully while the children giggle. "I can see why."

"They're always in high spirits for hours after he's left."

"Laughter is the best medicine, I guess." I glance at her with a smile. "Of course, what you do is good too."

She throws her head back, laughing. "Well thank you. We try our best." She shakes her head, dabbing a tissue at the corner of her eye. "I can see why he likes you."

"I'm glad someone can." I grin, holding my hand out to her. "I'm Marianne by the way."

"Nice to meet you, Marianne. I'm Maggie." She looks at me with her lips pulled to the side before nodding. "I think you'll be good for him." She reaches out, placing her hand on my arm. "Just treat him right." Her eyes fall back to Dallas clowning around. "He deserves some good in his life."

"He does, and I will." I push off the counter, brushing my hands down my front. "I'd better head in there."

She smiles warmly. "Okay. I'll be floating around if you need anything." Turning on silent feet, she makes her way down the corridor to do her rounds.

Dallas seems to sense my presence as I enter the ward because he turns and offers that gorgeous smile of his, and even though his floppy green wig and big red nose hide his face, I can still see those little crinkles beside his eyes. Those crinkles that, in this moment, make me appreciate how full of joy and laughter he is despite what he told me earlier.

"Well now, boys and girls," he says as he grabs my hand and pulls me in to the middle of the room with him. "I have a special friend for you to meet. This is Marianne."

I don't know why, but I curtsey. "How do you do?"

"Is she your girlfriend?" a little girl with her head wrapped in a scarf asks with a giggle.

In a big stage whisper behind his hand, he says, "I'm kinda hoping so." He glances back towards me with a wink. "If she'll have me."

"Are you kidding? How could I turn this down?" I sweep my hands through the air around him with a grin, and the children snicker. "Of course I'll be your girlfriend."

"Oooooh," they sing, then break into another bout of giggles.

Dallas chuckles, shaking his head. "Come on, I'll introduce you, and then you can read them some stories if you want." The lightbulb strikes. That's why I needed my glasses, not some weird fetish or kink he has.

He tugs on my hand, leading me to the bed with the little girl who spoke up. "This here is Missy and beside her is Sarah."

Missy looks up at me with her doe eyes and toothy grin. I offer my hand, and she looks to Dallas before accepting. "You're pretty," she says.

"And you're my new favourite person," I say with a grin. "You're very pretty too. I like your scarf."

Her hand flutters to her head, stroking the fabric fondly. "Thanks. I have a bunch of them, but this is my favourite one." She glances at Dallas then ducks her eyes and leans into me. "I always wear it on Saturdays." Her eyes flick back to him again, and a hint of pink colours her cheeks.

Sarah giggles. "Missy and Dallas up a tree," she sings quietly, and Missy's eyes go wide as she shushes her.

I grin knowingly. "It's okay. He *is* pretty dreamy." I point at the scarf she's wearing. "Hey, you think I would suit a scarf like that?"

She purses her lips, tapping her finger against her chin. "Hmm. Maybe, but you need a different colour to match your hair." Her eyes light up. "I've got just the one too." She crawls up to the head of her bed, opening the bedside drawer and rummaging around. "Here it is!" she says, triumphantly holding up a green one with white polka dots. "Here, you can borrow it."

Oh my heart.

"Thank you so much, but I don't know how to tie it. Do you think you could show me?"

She beams and her chest puffs out with pride. "It's really easy." She pats the bed for me to shift closer. I duck my head down, and she quickly wraps it over my head and ties it under my hair like a pro.

I sit up straight, twisting my head side to side. "How does it look?"

"Beautiful," she gushes.

"Not as beautiful as you, I'm sure."

"No one is as beautiful as Missy, right, kid?" Dallas winks as he comes to stand beside me, and her cheeks go a brighter shade of pink as she giggles. "Except maybe Sarah." He winks at her too. "Do you girls mind if I take Marianne away to meet the others?"

"Okay, but will you be back to visit again?" She blinks up at me with those bright expressive eyes.

"Just you try and stop me." I push up from the bed, pulling the scarf from my head to hand back.

Instead of reaching out for it, she studies it with a glint in her eyes. "No," she says, shaking her head and pushing my hand away. "You keep it. You can bring it back next Saturday." She settles back in her bed with a satisfied smirk.

"On one condition." I hold up a finger.

"What?"

Holding the scarf out to her, I wince apologetically. "You help me put it back on again."

Chapter Fourteen

"Make yourself at home. I won't be a minute." Dallas takes the stairs two at a time, somehow making it look effortless in those ridiculous pants he's wearing. Never in my wildest dreams did I ever picture myself checking out a clown, but the man certainly knows how to wear those oversized pants. There's probably room for two in them; a thought to revisit another day, when things have stepped up a notch or two between us.

Walking around his foyer, I trail my fingers along the small glass tabletop between two doors before peeking around the corner of one. I'm curious to see how he lives. Is he a neat freak? A messy slob? Does he have one of those talking fish hanging in his living room? God, I hope not.

I step into a beautifully rustic-looking kitchen that takes my breath away. It's like the man stepped inside my dreams and recreated it exactly. Right down to the deep ceramic sink, cast iron stove, and large wooden island that looks as though it doubles as a chopping block. There are even copper-bottomed pots hanging from a rack in the ceiling. Definitely not what I pictured for him, but at the same time, it suits him. I'm starting to realise there are many facets to this man I'm slowly becoming enamoured with.

Across from the kitchen is a table that looks as though it came straight from a fallen tree; all knobbly with jagged edges. Two matching weathered bench seats sit either side, and I'm reminded of a lodge we'd stayed in for school camp one year. The first time a boy held my hand was at a table much like this, and it brings a smile to my face just thinking about it. I can't resist taking a seat and running my hands along the oddly smooth surface of knotted wood as I survey the rest of the space.

Past the dining area is a lowered room with soft leather couches. An ornate fireplace takes up the wall opposite. There's no talking fish in sight, thank God, but there is an air of masculinity throughout the open-spaced room. It's all very Dallas. All except for one wall at the far end which takes my fancy. Bookshelves stuffed full of books stand either side of a beautiful bay window seat with cute fluffy pillows bunched in one corner. It looks like the perfect spot for curling up in the sunlight with a good book or trashy magazine. Something tells me it's where his wife used to sit, wiling away the time on a sunny afternoon, and a sadness fills my heart. They had a beautiful life here.

"Ready to go?" Dallas asks as he finds me still sitting at the table. I blink a few times to shoo away the tears that so easily come to the surface these days.

When I turn my gaze to him, I'm slightly taken aback. I've seen him with his white lab coat, and dressed in a suit for our dinner, and even as a clown, but there's something about seeing him in faded, well-fitted jeans that makes my insides turn to molten lava. He has a jacket slung over his arm, and his shirt sleeves are rolled up to reveal tanned forearms. Everyone knows a man is instantly a thousand times hotter when he does that. "Wow," is all I manage to utter as I push up from the table. My throat is suddenly drier than the Sahara, and at the same time feels as though I could drool all over the place.

His eyes follow me as I walk, and I pray to God I don't make an arse of myself and trip. That would be just my luck, falling arse over face in front of the man I'm trying so hard to impress.

He holds a hand out for me, and I take it, grateful for the stability. He inhales as his eyes rake over me appreciatively. "I really hope you meant what you said back at the hospital about being my girlfriend. I'd hate to disappoint Missy by showing up without you next week."

The uncertainty in his voice is endearing, and it makes me realise I'm not the only one feeling the effect of whatever is going on between us. I can't seem to find my equilibrium around him, especially when he's looking like a tasty snack with his sleeves the way they are. "I wouldn't dream of letting Missy down." I grin over my shoulder as I pull him towards the door. "And, you know, I kinda like you too."

He clutches a hand to his chest. "That has to be the nicest thing anyone has ever said to me before."

"Play your cards right, and there's more where that came from." I give him an exaggerated wink.

He sucks air in through his teeth. "I shall wait with bated breath."

"Where are we going, anyway?"

He holds up a finger, extricating himself from my grip as he backtracks to the kitchen. "I thought we could go for a walk in the park and have a picnic." He holds up a basket that just happened to be tucked away under the bench, and my insides go all squishy again.

Could this man be any more perfect?

"When did you have time to put this together?" I peer behind him. "Is there a secret maid in hiding somewhere back there?"

He chuckles, low and raspy. "Just a little something I prepared earlier."

"Well aren't you full of surprises today?"

"Just trying to return the favour." He winks. "You certainly surprised me the first day we met."

My eyes widen briefly before I erupt into giggles. "Well as long as we're surprising each other, I guess things will stay interesting between us. Though I can't promise I'll surprise you *that* much again." I stretch up on tippy toes to plant a soft kiss on his lips, then his cheek, inhaling his musky scent as I do. A tiny sigh escapes my lips as I pull away.

"Did you just sniff me?"

"If you're going to wear cologne that smells delicious, you have to be prepared to be sniffed. It's my right as the girlfriend." I screw my nose up. "Ugh. That just doesn't sound right. Am I too old to be a girlfriend? I feel like I'm too old. But we can't go around saying we're *lovers* either." I shudder. "That word is even worse."

"First of all, you can never be too old to be a girlfriend. Second, you're hardly what I would call old. And third, what's wrong with the word lovers?"

"Eww don't." I cringe. "It's just wrong. Plus, we haven't even done anything to equate being—I can't believe I'm saying it again—*lovers.*" An involuntary shiver runs down my spine. "As for me being old, I think you'll find that under all this guff," I gesture to my made-up face, "and the hair dye, lies an old, old lady."

He shakes his head, linking his fingers through mine as he leads me back towards the door. "I'm not buying it for a second. You could let your hair go au naturel, scrub the make-up off your face, or even dress up as a clown if you so desired, and I'd still think you're beautiful."

"I feel like that's a challenge."

He shrugs, smirking. "It's really not. I don't care what you look like on the outside. It's what's in here that counts." He places a hand across my heart, and I swear it skips a beat. "So if you *feel* like you could be my girlfriend, then you're my girlfriend. If not, we'll coin our own phrase for it."

I do like the sound of that. I also like the sound of him. "How is this real right now?"

"What do you mean?"

"This. You. You say all these things and you make me feel… I don't know, like I'm something amazing."

"Because you are."

"You say that now, but when I let my grey hair grow out and stop getting manicures and wearing make-up, will you really still see it that way?"

Dallas shakes his head, a frown marring his perfect face. "I don't know what he said to you to make you think you need all this," he trails a finger down my cheek, "to be beautiful. The person inside is beautiful already, and that's the person I'm interested in."

"Okay, well if you really don't care… then I might just stop doing it." I watch him for a reaction but there isn't one.

"Whatever makes you happy."

I reach up and press my lips to his. "You make me happy. That's all I need." I smile, turning on my heels. "Plus, it'll save me a *lot* of money. Looking this good doesn't come cheap."

Chapter Fifteen

"Let me get this straight. You're going to stop dying your hair and wearing make-up to prove that you're an old lady?" Susan tilts her head to the side, pursing her lips. "I don't get it."

At this point, neither do I. No matter what the outcome, I can't win. Me and my stupid big mouth. "I'm doomed, aren't I?" I let my head hang in defeat.

"I mean, it's not how I would've played it, but each to their own, I guess." She shrugs. "More wine?"

I roll my eyes towards her. "It's Saturday night. Of course I want more wine." I tilt my glass forward, and she promptly fills it to the brim.

"Atta girl. Let wine fix your problems like the rest of us." She cackles, leaning back on the couch and kicking her feet up on the coffee table. "You know what we need to do to take your mind off all this?"

"Stock up on hair dye for when I come to my senses?"

"Uh, duh, but that's not what I was talking about." She holds her glass up, pointing her pinkie finger out at me. "Someone is having a big birthday soon," she sings, waggling her eyebrows as a grin spreads across her face.

"Like I need reminding." I rub a hand down my face, peering up at her through my fingers. "How exactly is that taking my mind off the fact I'm an old lady?"

She snorts and rolls her eyes until her eyelashes flutter. "Forty is not old! I should know," she points at herself, "forty-one right here, remember?"

"Yeah, but you're you."

She screws her nose up as if there's a bad taste in her mouth. "And you're you. What's your point?"

I wave my hand in her direction. "Where do I start? Not a grey hair on your head, not a wrinkle in sight, and barely an ounce of fat on you. You could pass for a twenty-something easily."

"Firstly, thank you." She pats her hair and sucks her cheeks in. "But I could *never* pass for twenty. Have you hung out with someone in their twenties lately?" She widens her eyes dramatically, making herself comfortable. "Just hearing them talk is exhausting. I mean, it's like they have a whole other dialogue. Words we used to know mean different things now. I can't keep up with them. All that crazy talk and… energy." She practically spits the word then shudders. "It's just unnatural."

"Makes me tired just thinking about it."

"Mmhmm. Why hasn't anyone figured out how to bottle that shit up yet? We could put it to much better use." She grins. "Like celebrating your birthday!" She tucks her legs underneath her and wiggles her hips. "Let's have a party!"

"Did you miss the part about us being old and tired?"

"Ugh, don't be a party pooper. You only turn forty once, and as your best friend, I refuse to let it go by without a proper celebration."

"But—"

"Nope. Not a word. It's happening." I know better than to try and deny her. She'll only dig her heels in and make a big song and dance about it. It's easier to just let her have her way.

"Fine." I draw the word out on a sigh. "But nothing too flashy, okay? Just a few friends out for a meal and drinks. Something laid back. I hear Tui has her own place now. Maybe we could see if we can use that," I suggest weakly.

"I don't think you understand. I said party. P. A. R. T. Y. You know, loud music, dancing, cocktails, the whole shebang!" I raise an eyebrow at her, and she bounces on the couch as she takes hold of my arm in a vicelike grip. "Come on," she whines, "you can let your hair down for one night." Her bottom lip drops, and she brings out the big guns. "Pleeeeeeaaaaase?"

I roll my eyes so hard my head flops back against the couch. "Okay, okay. We can have a party."

"Yes! You won't have to lift a finger, I promise. I'll organise the whole thing."

"That's what I'm afraid of," I groan.

She grabs her phone and starts clicking away, her tongue sticking out the side of her mouth as she nods and mumbles to herself. Clearly the wheels are already in motion and I'm no longer required for this conversation. It'd almost be amusing if it wasn't my party she was organising, but my stomach fills with dread at the thought of all the debauchery she could have in store for me. I should probably prewarn Dallas. He's never had the full Susan experience, and I don't want him scared off. Not when things are going so great between us.

"I know that look." She grins at me while her fingers continue typing away on her phone like they're possessed. It takes some skill to be able to multitask at that level. "You're thinking about him again, aren't you?"

I feel my cheeks redden as I trail a finger around the rim of my glass. "You saw him. Can you blame me?"

"No, no I cannot. I still can't believe you haven't licked that man from head to toe already." She licks her lips. "I know I would've."

"Well you can keep your tongue in your own mouth, thank you very much. He's mine."

"Ooh, possessive much?" She giggles, downing the last of her glass before reaching for the bottle. "You know I'm just playing. I would never get in the way of your hooha getting some much-needed loving. Speaking of which, have you made sure the downstairs is in ship-shape condition, ready for the big reveal? Waxed and vajazzled and what not?"

I nearly spit my wine across the room but manage to choke it down between giggles. "I am *not* vajazzling my hooha for anyone!" I shake my head, still giggling. "You make it sound like a sordid game show, you know. The big reveal."

"I mean, it can be." She waggles her brows. "If that's what you're into."

"It's been so long between… *reveals*, I don't even know what I'm into anymore. Or if I was ever into anything in the first place."

Susan sticks out her bottom lip, rubbing a hand up and down my arm. "Aww, honey. I knew Ernie was a selfish prick, but you never said he was a dud in the bedroom." She shakes her head, placing her glass on the table. "All those wasted years."

"I don't know that he was a dud. He just liked it a particular way, every time. And he wasn't very… experimental."

She throws her head back, snoring. "The exact same way every single time? Damn." She levels me with a stare. "And this particular way of his, did it take care of *your* needs too?" One eyebrow lifts as she purses her lips.

"I mean, sometimes. If I really focused." I cringe and cover my face with my hands as I say it because I know how bad it sounds. Peeking through my fingers, I can see that Susan is none too pleased with it either.

Her eyebrows just about hit the ceiling, and she gets up on her knees, her hands held in a sort of prayer-like pose. "If you really focused?" She speaks each word slowly as if it hurts to even say the words. "What happened to hot and heavy? Where's the romance? The passion?" She throws her hands in the air. "I can't believe you've had nothing but bad sex for years! That's just not okay." Leaping off the couch with a surprising amount of grace, she heads for the kitchen.

"Where are you going?"

"We're gonna need a lot more wine for this conversation." She comes back in with two bottles held in the air. "A lot."

"All because I had crappy sex? I wish I'd told you sooner." I snort, holding my glass out for a refill.

"I wish you had too. I'd have dragged your sorry arse to the bars with me until I knew you'd had a jolly good rogering if I'd known." She shakes her head and gives me the side eye. "Life's much too short to be having shitty sex, or no sex, for that matter."

Taking a large gulp of my wine, I settle back against the couch, and my mind instantly falls back to Dallas. If the way he kisses is anything to go by, I don't think I'll have anything to worry about in the sex department.

"You're doing it again." She pokes my arm with a cheesy grin before turning her eyes skyward. "Please, dear God, let Doctor Hottie be the sexual awakening my friend so desperately needs. And I mean *desperately*."

I nudge her with my foot. "I'm not *that* desperate." She turns her face to me, dropping her chin and looking at me like I'm deranged. "I'm not!"

"You wait." She nods with a smug look on her face. "You just wait until you get a decent bit of vitamin D in your diet. Then you'll understand. There'll be no going back from that." She shakes her head. "Nope. No going back."

Chapter sixteen

My head throbs along to the beat of my heart as I stare at my bedraggled reflection in the mirror. Half my hair hangs in thick clumps while the rest is plastered to the side of my face, and I re-evaluate my decision to let Susan convince me to put warm olive oil in my hair last night. In my vino-addled state, I had believed her when she said it would strip the colour out and leave my hair looking luxuriously moisturised and natural.

It did not.

Although, by that stage, we had polished off bottle number four, so it's anyone's guess as to how she even got this idea in the first place. All I know is, my hair looks worse than it did with its 2cm regrowth, and I now smell like a chip shop.

I down a couple of Panadol with a large glass of water, then reach into the shower to get the water running. Surely if I have it hot enough, the oil will slide right out of my hair and down the drain, which is more than I can say for my pillowcases. The only place they'll be sliding down is the rubbish bin.

I tip my head back to rinse out the last of the conditioner and note that it already feels a damn sight better than it did when I first stepped under the water. Maybe I won't have to wear a sack on my head until I can get to the salon.

Stepping out of the shower, I towel myself dry before tentatively moving towards the mirror. With a deep breath, I lean forward and swipe a hand across the fog so I can see myself. What I see is not quite what I expected, but in a good way. My hair no longer hangs in clumps, and I still have my red tresses but dotted throughout are streaks of grey and white. It almost looks trendy. I can't believe it worked!

With a bounce in my step, I don my comfy jeans and a long-sleeved tee then pull my hair up into a messy bun, leaving a few tendrils to frame my face. The reflection in the mirror is not too shabby. In fact, there's a brightness in my eyes despite the raging hangover, and I believe I have a certain someone to thank for that, and I don't mean Susan.

The question is, will he let me thank him in the way I want to?

###

"You're looking radiant this morning, Marianne," Dallas says as he ushers me inside. "There's something different about you today." He taps a finger against his chin as his eyes scour over me. Holding my arms out to my sides, I do a slow spin then face him with a grin. "Have you done something different with your hair?" He brings a hand up to brush the loose strands behind my ear, and I press my cheek into his palm. "It looks nice."

"How very perceptive of you. And us only on our—" I tilt my head to the side as I count, "—fourth date. That's quite impressive."

Cupping his hand under my jaw, he tilts my face up to plant a soft kiss on my lips. "I have every one of your features committed to memory. How could I not notice?" It takes everything I have not to jump his bones right now. Seriously, what man on the face of the planet has ever noticed a change in hairstyle or colour?

Frowning, I shrug. "I guess I'm not used to it, is all."

"Well, get used to it." He points to his chest with a wink. "I'm a doctor. I'm trained to notice things. Occupational hazard."

"I wouldn't call it a hazard. It's nice to know all the effort I put in isn't for nothing." I gesture to the vintage jeans I'm wearing, complete with frayed bottoms from being stood on. The joys of being on the shorter side. "This kinda style doesn't just come naturally, you know." I flick my head, placing a hand on my hip. "I'll have you know it took a whole fifteen minutes to get this look right."

His eyes bug out. "Fifteen? Phew," he says with a shake of his head. "That's some preparation time right there." He gestures to his own jeans and shirt then holds up his hand, fingers spread out. "Five minutes, and that includes my hair." He mimics my head toss before raking a hand through his silver locks with a grin.

Placing a hand across my heart, I bat my eyes. "All that effort for little ol' me?"

"Only the best for my girlfriend." He waggles his eyebrows in amusement as I inwardly cringe. It's still weird hearing that word. *Girlfriend.* I don't think I'll ever get used to it.

"So, what movie are we seeing?" I purse my lips, tapping a finger against my chin. "Let me guess, you're into those artsy type films with the subtitles and deep meanings. I see you as a *Good Will Hunting* man, or maybe a *Crouching Tiger, Hidden Dragon* kinda guy."

He raises a brow, smirking. "If by artsy you mean cult classics like *Back to the Future*, then yes, you're spot on."

"Woah, this is heavy. That's my favourite movie too!" I giggle, completely taken by surprise. This man never ceases to amaze me. Never in a million years would I have pegged him for a Marty McFly fan.

"Great Scott!" He shakes his head with an amused expression. "Gorgeous *and* she has great taste in movies. You're the woman of my dreams." He clasps my hand, bringing it to his lips, and I swoon just a little more. "I have to admit, I stereotypically thought you'd be into the romance genre of film. I should've known you'd have a more eclectic taste."

"Don't get me wrong, I love a good romcom or ugly-cry film, but you can't beat a bit of cheesy over-the-top fun."

"Ugly cry?"

"Yeah, you know, the kind of soul-destroying story that makes you sob relentlessly so your face ends up all red and blotchy." I shrug. "Ugly cry."

"Why would you want to subject yourself to that kind of torture?"

"Umm, because sometimes you just need a good cry. It's very therapeutic."

"I'll have to take your word for it." He waves a hand forward. "Shall we?"

"We shall." I follow him outside and wait as he locks the door, taking the time to admire the view from behind. He really does wear those jeans well.

He spins to face me, clearing his throat with a grin, and I realise he's caught me checking him out. I lift my chin, meeting his eye with a smirk, and he chuckles. "I was planning on taking you to some soppy 'chick flick', but now that I know what you like, I don't suppose you'd want to see the new *Bill and Ted* movie instead? It just came out today."

I can't contain the smile that wants to break free. He couldn't be any more perfect if he tried. "Keanu Reeves and a trip down memory lane? Duuuude, of course I would." I poke my tongue between my teeth and do my best air guitar impression.

He nods enthusiastically, putting on a surfer accent. "Most excellent, and might I say, you have epic guitar skills."

I nod, blowing across my knuckles. "What can I say? I've been practising for years."

"Oh, it shows." His eyes light up as he takes my hand in his. "You're really something else, you know that?"

"A good something, I hope."

"The *best* something. I'm really glad our friends pushed us into this dating thing."

I nudge his arm with my shoulder. "I'm glad too. I guess they know us better than we know ourselves."

"I guess so." He checks his watch. "We've got plenty of time until the movie starts. Do you feel like walking into town?"

I couldn't think of a single thing I'd like more. Anything to keep his hand in mine. "Yeah, I'd like that."

Chapter seventeen

"That was so much better than I expected it to be." I giggle, threading my arm through Dallas's as we leave the theatre. "I don't think I've laughed so much through a movie in a while."

"Perhaps you should stop going to those ugly-cry films you mentioned and try more comedies." He nudges my side, smirking. "Much better for the soul."

"Hey, there's something soul cleansing about a good cry, I'll have you know. It's kind of like hitting a reset button."

"That's how I feel about going to the children's hospital. It somehow takes away any negative feelings I've been holding onto and, like you said, I guess it resets me." He stares off into the distance, a look of peace washing over his face.

"You really love those kids, don't you?"

He flicks his gaze to mine, the deep-seated emotion shining through. "It's hard not to. They're great kids."

"They are." I nod, peering up at him with a lump in my throat. "You would've made a wonderful father, you know? I'm so sorry you had that taken away from you."

He averts his gaze, his head bobbing slowly. "Thank you."

There's so much pain and anguish in those two words, and I wish with all my heart I could ease his suffering somehow. I can't imagine how hard that must have been to go through on his own. It certainly puts all my worries into perspective. Yes, I'm getting older, but at least I get that opportunity. Not everyone is granted the same.

Giving his arm a squeeze, I lead him to a bench seat underneath a tree. With tentative fingers, I graze his cheek before cupping his face and bringing it to face me. "What can I do?" I search his eyes, smoothing the crease on his forehead.

"You're already doing it." He smiles, taking my hand in his and pressing his lips to the tips of my fingers. "Showing me life is still worth living."

I gasp, my heart racing. "Please—"

He holds his hand up, shaking his head with a chuckle. "Sorry. I didn't mean it like that."

Clasping a hand to my chest, I huff out a breath. "Oh, thank God. You had me worried there. You can't go saying things like that. You'll give me a heart attack."

"Sorry." He squeezes my hand. "I only mean that before you came along, I wasn't really living. After Clarissa died, I threw myself into work and volunteering with the children, and I guess I forgot to live my own life." He rakes a hand through his hair. "I guess a part of me died along with them, and I never really allowed myself to live."

"Because she never got the chance," I finish for him. "I can understand that. Hell, I did the same after Ernie, and he's still here to haunt me." I wince, throwing a hand across my mouth. "Oh my god, I can't believe I just said that. I didn't mean that she was haunting you or anything."

Dallas chuckles, threading his fingers through mine. "It's fine. I knew what you meant."

Resting my head on his shoulder, I snort. "Now's probably a good time to tell you I suffer from a foot-in-mouth affliction. In case you hadn't already figured that out from my outstanding conversation skills."

"I enjoy your conversation. There's never a dull moment with you." He kisses my head while his thumb traces circles across the back of my hand. "Maybe that's why we found each other. I needed your bright light to help me see in the dark, and you needed to see yourself through my eyes."

I lift my head to rest my chin on his shoulder and watch him with a quirk of my brow. "Did you, a man of science, just admit to believing in fate?"

"I don't know about fate, but—"

"Destiny?" I offer with a grin.

"Now you're pushing it. Can't we just be two people who saw a need in each other?"

"How very romantic." I roll my eyes. "That doesn't explain how out of all the doctors in this town, you ended up being the one on call when I had my little incident, *or* how we both had busy body friends who pushed us into dating, *or* how we ended up matched on HookUp.com.”

“Coincidence. Right place at the right time.”

“Or,” I draw out the word, “fate.”

He throws his head back, a smirk tugging at his lips. “Alright, fine,” he concedes. “Maybe there was a little bit of fate involved.” He holds his finger and thumb together. “A tiny bit.”

“Well, whatever it was, fate or otherwise, I’m pretty glad it happened.”

“Me too.”

Chapter eighteen

"You two are so adorable. I love that he's into all those cheesy movies you like. Gets me off the hook." Susan swipes a hand across her forehead in mock relief. Grabbing the bag of popcorn from the microwave, she pours it into a bowl before joining me on the couch. "I really don't see the appeal."

"Come on, they're good fun."

"If you say so." She rolls her eyes. "I'd much rather watch something with a bit of heat in it. Speaking of which, have you heard about that new movie on Netflix? Three hundred and something days?"

"365 perhaps?"

"Yeah, something like that." She waves a hand through the air. "I've heard it's off the charts hot. Like *Fifty Shades* but next level." She waggles her eyebrows as she throws a piece of popcorn into her mouth, crunching down loudly. "We should totally watch it."

"Suz, you know I love you, but I really don't think I want to watch a sex movie with you." I inwardly cringe. *Awkward.*

"Oh, don't be such a prude! You might pick up a few tricks to use on the doc."

"Oh my god, no! We haven't even had regular sex yet. I'm not about to pull out some kinky moves and scare him off."

"First of all, you're so vanilla it's not even funny. *Regular* sex. It's just sex, sweetheart. No one calls it 'regular' sex." She shakes her head. "And I don't know what you're so worried about. He clearly knows what you get up to behind closed doors. He helped you pull a foreign object out of your vajayjay, remember? If that didn't scare him off, I don't think you have anything to worry about. Even the most vanilla of men would be turned on knowing you had something kinky up your sleeves."

Grabbing a handful of popcorn, I settle back on the couch, cocking my head with a grin. "I have to put things up my sleeves now? Jesus, sex *has* changed." I snort, and a piece of popcorn comes flying at my head. "Hey! You could've poked my eye out with that."

"Oh please. Cry me a river." She pouts before throwing another piece in my direction.

"Now you're just wasting food."

"It's true. I am." She picks up another piece, tossing it up and down in her hand. "But you know what would make me stop?"

I sigh, flopping my head back against the couch. "Watching the sexy film?"

"Hey now, there's an idea. Thanks for suggesting it." A devilish grin spreads across her face as she grabs the remote and starts pushing buttons.

"Okay, but I'm going to need wine for this. There's no way I'm watching porn with you while sober." I push up from the couch and make my way into the kitchen for a bottle and two glasses.

"Now we're talking. You do know I get super horny after a few wines though, right?" She cackles, thrusting her hips up off the couch.

"I think *everyone* knows that fact about you, Suz. And with your current dry spell, you'd probably get turned on by *Postman Pat* or a gentle breeze." I snort. "Just remember to use the spare room down the hall if you're going to stay. I don't need to hear that *again*." A shudder runs down my spine as I recall the last time she stayed over and had a little 'alone time'.

"So I get a little vocal." She shrugs. "I like to give myself encouragement."

I bark out a laugh. "Is that what they're calling it these days? Sounded more like you were cheering on the whole damn neighbourhood." Uncapping the wine, I pour two large glasses before settling back on the couch.

"You know what they say, sharing is caring. Just doing my bit and sharing a bit of love with the community."

"I'm sure they really appreciated it," I say with a roll of my eyes. I tuck my feet beneath me and drag a cushion over to nestle against. "Alright. Let's get this thing over with."

As the closing credits roll up the screen, I find myself squirming in my seat. I'm sure my face is beet-red. I just watched something akin to an extended porno, and I'm all kinds of turned on right now, which is wrong on so many levels considering I've got a few wines under my belt and my best friend is sitting beside me, her eyes boring into the side of my head.

Fanning my face, I clear my throat, unable to meet Suz's gaze. "Well, that was... an experience."

She snorts out a laugh, tipping the last of her wine down her throat. "I think the word you're looking for is hot."

I manage to peek up at her then erupt into a fit of giggles. "It really was. But that ending though." I level her with a stare, and she grins.

"Yeah, sorry, I should've warned you it ended on a cliff hanger. It's all anyone could talk about on social media for weeks. Well, that and the epic sex scenes."

"Do you… do you think they were really doing it? Like for real? Because it definitely didn't look like any romance I've ever seen before."

She grins, waggling her brows at me. "God, I hope so." She licks her lips then slaps her hands down on her thighs, pushing up off the couch. "I don't know about you, but I'm heading up for some me time." She chortles, sauntering towards the stairs. "You might want to use your earplugs."

Ewww. She's my best friend, and I love her, but I'll be damned if I'm going to sit down the hall and listen to that again. Once was more than enough.

Settling back into the couch, I drag the throw rug over my legs. May as well get comfortable, I could be here for a while.

Chapter nineteen

I've been practising my scarf-tying technique all week, even watching a few YouTube tutorials so I can show Missy when we go to the hospital this morning. I think I've become rather proficient at it now, and I can't wait to show her what I've learned. I even bought us a matching set – red with vanilla cupcakes for her and blue with chocolate ones for me. There's something so charming about that little girl, and I want her to like me. She's got this quiet confidence about her, like that of someone much older, and she's oh so smitten with Dallas; not that I can blame her. And it's obvious how much she means to him too. I suppose I'd like to win her over, have her seal of approval.

Dallas pulls up to the curb, and I saunter down the path to meet him. This time he's wearing a purple wig and has bright red suspenders holding up baggy, polka-dot pants. A pair of oversized shoes sit on the seat beside him, and he quickly throws them in the back as I climb in.

"Looking good there, doc." I wink as I reach over and honk his fluffy red nose. "Is it weird that I find this look attractive?"

His laugh bellows out. "Maybe a little. But it's better than being petrified of it." He pulls the car out and heads down the road. "There was one nurse, when I first started volunteering, who went pale as a ghost when I walked in dressed like this. She stumbled backwards until she hit the wall behind her. I had to take the wig and nose off before she could calm down enough to speak."

"Oh, the poor thing. What happened to her?"

He chuckles. "She ended up requesting a transfer to the afternoon shift."

"Aww, you scary brute." I grin, nudging his arm. "She was probably having flashbacks of Pennywise."

Dallas clutches a hand to his chest. "You wound me. I'm not that scary, am I?"

I purse my lips, taking my time to look him up and down with a smirk. "No, I don't think so. Maybe if you walked in carrying a red balloon…"

He shakes his head, chuckling. "I may have been wearing a red wig at the time, but I would never do *that*."

"Yeah, probably not the best idea to show up to a children's hospital dressed as the clown from everyone's nightmares." I gesture to his clothes. "I mean, what you've gone with would most definitely be someone's *fashion* nightmare, but I kinda dig it."

"So, no clown phobias for you then?"

"Not really, no. Don't get me wrong, if I was walking down the road by myself and there was a clown standing on the side of the road carrying a red balloon, I'd likely wet my pants as I ran away screaming, but your general run of the mill clown is fine with me." I reach a finger under the strap of his suspenders and tug. "And, like I said, I find it oddly attractive on you." I pull my lip in between my teeth. Who am I kidding? He could be wearing a sack and I'd find him attractive. That damn movie has been playing on my mind all week, and I've been having extremely vivid dreams featuring the silver fox before me.

"More attractive than regular me?" he asks with an amused look on his face.

I hold my hands up. "All I'm saying is, I wouldn't kick either of you out of bed."

His cheeks redden through the white face paint, and a satisfied grin pulls at my lips. He clears his throat, shifting in his seat. "Good to know."

I take his hand, placing it on my thigh. "Did I just make the good doctor blush?"

He clears his throat again before laughing under his breath. He turns his eyes skyward as he says, "Give me strength."

"For me?" Missy's mouth hangs agape as she accepts my carefully wrapped gift.

"Sure is." I watch as she slowly peels the Sellotape from the paper piece by piece. When she gathers the fabric in her tiny hands, I pull the other one out of my bag and hold it out for her to see. "I got us matching ones."

She squeals in delight, clambering onto her knees to get a closer look. "They're beautiful."

"They'll be even more beautiful on." I grin, taking mine and deftly tying it around my head, this time knotting it at the front.

Missy sucks in a breath. "You've been practising." Tugging her own scarf from her head, she holds her new one out to me. "Can you show me? Please?" She casts a glance around the room, seeking out Dallas's mop of purple curls. "I want to look pretty, like you."

Tears form in my eyes as I take her hands in mine. "Oh, honey, you're already pretty."

A tinge of pink colours her cheeks and she ducks her head, peeking up at me. "You think so?"

"Are you kidding? Why do you think I practised this scarf tying so much?" I gesture to the knot sitting atop my head. "So *I* could be as pretty as *you*."

She grins wide. "I do rock a scarf."

"You do."

Her smile fades as she reaches up to touch the wispy hair still left on her head. "But you look pretty even without a scarf."

I blink away the tears still threatening and perch on the side of the bed, pulling her into me. "Please don't think you need to cover yourself up to be beautiful, Missy." With a finger under her chin, I tip her face to meet my gaze. "Beauty is so much more than skin deep, and you, my darling girl, radiate beauty."

"But boys like girls to be pretty and have long flowing hair."

"Oh, honey, not every boy is like that." My eyes find Dallas's across the room, and he raises his brow in question. I give him a nod and smile. "The good ones don't care about things like that. They don't care if you have long hair or short hair, because they see what's inside." And just like that, a weight is lifted from my shoulder as I fully accept what Dallas has been telling me all along. I *am* more than my looks.

"I guess that makes sense." She nods, her fingers reaching out to tangle in one of my wayward curls. "It'd still be nice to have long hair though."

I lean in conspiratorially. "Long hair is overrated. Trust me."

Chapter twenty

Rolling out of bed, I pad down to the kitchen for a much-needed coffee and breakfast. I flick the jug on and go about making some toast with plain old marmite, not able to stomach anything more than that with my tummy tied in knots. I'm meeting Dallas this morning, showing him a more vulnerable side to me. A side I've let slip into the background for the better part of five years. And something I've regretted ever since.

But after the way Dallas opened up to me last weekend, and my conversation with Missy yesterday, I feel it's finally time to embrace that side once more. It's time to open myself up to being vulnerable, and I'm scared as hell.

When I got home from the hospital yesterday, I called an old friend who owns a bakery in town. She owes me a favour, and I'm finally redeeming it. We haven't seen each other since my marriage went tits up, but when we spoke on the phone, it was as if we'd never stopped, and she was all for helping me out. If anyone can understand why this is so important to me, it's Tui. After all, she went through it with me.

I've always loved experimenting in the kitchen, and for as long as I can remember, it had been a dream of mine to one day own a boutique patisserie. I'd even enrolled in a school for pastry arts, but Ernie had other ideas of what I should do. *"Pastry chef? No one makes money baking cakes, Marianne. All you'll get out of that is fat."* Then he'd laughed and pointed me in the direction of office management instead because that was a 'good solid job'. When I look back now, I can't believe I let him belittle me that way, but I guess that's how it started. Small 'jokes' to keep me in line and doing what he wanted. Pokes and prods to suggest I wasn't at my best for him. And then the icing on the cake; the betrayal of his affair, and the gall he had to blame it on me.

Well, he's someone else's problem now, and even though it's taken me three years to do so, I think I'm ready to find some semblance of my former self and follow my dreams. Seeing Dallas with those children at the hospital was a reminder that we only have such a short time on this earth, so we may as well make the most of it and do what we're called to do.

###

"How do you feel about getting your hands dirty today?" I link my arm through his then entwine our fingers.

He wiggles his free hand in the air. "Doctor, remember? Getting dirty is an everyday occurrence for me." I know he's talking about blood and other gross stuff, but my mind chooses to go down a different path.

"Oh, is it now, Doctor Mahoney? I do like a man who's not afraid to get down and dirty," I purr, surprising even myself. "Perhaps, after our date, we can get... more dirty... together?" I let my awkward question linger in the air as I turn what I hope are coquettish eyes to Dallas.

He swallows visibly, his jaw pulled tight as his eyes darken, and I almost tell him to flag the whole date and instead take me up to his room and ravage me, but I manage to compose myself. Just.

Instead of ripping his shirt off like my fingers are itching to do, I settle for smoothing my hands down his chest, noting the firm ridges beneath his crisp navy shirt. His hands find mine and place them around his waist as he takes my lips in a heated kiss that takes my breath away. "Yes. I'd very much like to get dirty with you, Marianne." His voice is gruff and strained, and it sets my insides on fire. I did that to him. Even with my bumbling awkwardness, I made him want me.

"I'm going to hold you to that, doc."

Chapter twenty-one

"Marianne!" Tui holds her arms out to her sides as she rushes towards me. "*Haere mai*, girl." She pulls me into a fierce hug. "It's been forever and a day. Let me look at you." She holds me at arm's length, her lips pursed as she looks me up and down. "I love the glasses."

My hand automatically reaches up to adjust them at the mention. "Thanks."

"You've lost weight too."

"A little." She quirks her brow at me, folding her arms across her ample chest. "What? I had some to lose." I brush my hands down my front and avert my eyes. Like me, Tui is a feeder; someone who likes to make sure people are looked after. She tsks at me, and I meet her eye. "I did, and I'm fine. Honestly." I glance at Dallas, standing by watching us, and I can't help but grin. "I'm happy."

Tui flicks her eyes between Dallas and I before a smile slowly spreads across her face. "If you're happy, I'm happy." She bustles us through the door, flipping the closed sign over and snibbing the lock.

"Oh, I hope you're not closing the shop just for us."

"On one of my best sale days? Girl, you crazy." Tui laughs, shaking her head. "I love you and all, but I'm not about to lose takings so you can win over lover boy over here." She hooks a thumb towards Dallas with a cheeky grin, and he chuckles. "Even if he is cute."

I grin. I can't believe I let myself forget how easy it was to be around Tui. Yet another ball I seem to have let drop after my world came crashing down.

"I've got my girls opening up in about an hour, so we best get to work. Through here." She ushers us into the kitchen. "I still don't understand what you need me for, but I'm glad you called me, Marianne. It's been far too long between visits."

"I know. I'm sorry. I became somewhat of a hermit after... well, you know.... and then time just slipped on by." I shake my head, knowing it's a poor excuse for neglecting my friends, but it's the truth. If it wasn't for Susan forcing her way into my home every weekend, I don't think I would've seen anyone outside of work.

"Don't I know it. Time has not been kind." She lifts her knee and taps it. "It's never been right since I had my op, and the damn thing seizes up when rain's coming." She chuckles. "But at least I don't have to bother with the weather channel anymore!"

Trust Tui to find the silver lining. She always was one of those glass-half-full people. "No, I suppose you wouldn't."

"*You* look well though. You're practically glowing. And I'm guessing this one," she gestures to Dallas, "is why you look so damn happy. Am I right?"

"I'd like to think so," Dallas says, stepping forward and offering his hand. "Dallas Mahoney."

"*Doctor* Dallas Mahoney," I correct, giving Tui a wink.

She tilts her head with a nod of approval. "Well okay then. I'm Tui, like the bird, or the beer." She winks. "And I'm pleased to see this one with a smile on her face. It's been a minute." She steps in behind me, whispering, "You done good, girl," under her breath as she passes, and I can't help but giggle.

"Thanks. I think I'll keep him." The raised eyebrow he gives me only makes me laugh even harder.

"So, what are you two lovebirds wanting to learn that you don't already know, hmm?" Tui lifts an apron over her head, pulling it tight and fastening it at the back. "There ain't a damn thing I can make you can't make better." She hands us each an apron as she nods at Dallas. "She cooked for you yet?"

He leans back against the bench and crosses one foot over the other, "No, she hasn't." He looks to me then back at her. "What am I missing?"

"You haven't told him? *Auē*," she scolds as she flicks the corner of her apron at me.

"I don't know what you're talking about; there's nothing to tell. And I'm cooking for him tonight, if you must know. That's why we're here; so you can help us make some bread to go with it," I say indignantly. She's making it into a much bigger deal than it is.

"Why do I feel like there's a story in here?" Dallas leans over, nudging me with his elbow. "What aren't you telling me?"

Tui fixes me with a look. "You and I both know you don't need to be here to learn how to make bread."

Dallas turns to me with questioning eyes.

"It's nothing." I wave my hand through the air.

"It's more than nothing." Tui gestures to the spacious kitchen and storefront. "None of this would be possible if it wasn't for you giving up your spot." Her voice softens as she takes my hand. "I never would've considered going to Petit Patisserie if it wasn't for you taking me under your wing and teaching me all you knew. You were always there cheering me on." She frowns. "Even when it should've been you in my place, you never stopped encouraging me."

"That's what friends are for." I realise the irony of my words; I haven't exactly been the best friend I could be. When things turned to shit with Ernie, I'd pulled back from everyone, not wanting to make them 'choose a side'. I guess I'd assumed everyone would pick him.

"You wanted to be a pastry chef?" Dallas asks, and I nod.

"I did. Still do, if I'm honest."

"What stopped you?"

"More like *who*." Tui flicked a tea towel over her shoulder with a scowl. "Just because he was jealous that you were so good at something he couldn't understand, didn't mean he had to squash your dreams like that."

"It's not entirely his fault. I should've stood up for myself." I shake my head. "I think back now and I can't believe I let him treat me the way he did, but that's the thing. I did let him. I got in my own way."

"He took advantage of your good nature, that's what he did." She pokes a finger at my chest. "And he robbed the world of the epic culinary skills of Marianne Archer."

I roll my eyes. "That's going a bit far."

She turns her eyes to Dallas. "Let's let him be the judge of that, shall we? You just wait, bro, she's gonna knock your socks off."

He holds his hands in the air. "You don't have to tell me. She already knocks my socks off."

Tui rocks back on her heels. "Hoo, he is a charmer, this one, ain't he?"

I slip my arm around his, resting my chin on his shoulder. "He sure is. And I kinda like it."

###

"Punch it!" Tui grips one side of the bowl in front of her and punches the dough with her other hand. She pulls the edges to the centre and removes it from the bowl, placing it on the floured board. "Give it a light knead, just one or two goes to release the air pockets, then shape it into a ball."

Dallas and I follow her instructions before placing our dough balls onto a baking tray with cornmeal scattered over it. We give it a light brush with oil, then cover it again and leave it to rise once more.

"Another coffee while we wait it out?" Tui dusts her floured hands down her apron front before pulling it over her head and heading out to the shop. The coffee machine whirs to life once more as we take a seat at one of the tables in the busy bakery. There's a lot of hustle and bustle for a Sunday morning.

"You have flour on your face," Dallas says as he reaches out and lightly dusts his thumb across my cheek. I lean into his touch, humming as I close my eyes. When I open them, he's watching me with a small smile on his face. "You seem so at ease here."

"That's because I am." I smile, leaning back in my seat. "The kitchen has always been my happy place. Cooking, baking. This is what I always wanted to do." I gesture to the room around us. "Run my own bakery."

"You would be brilliant at it."

I laugh. "You haven't even tried anything I've made yet."

"No, but I can tell by the way you move in the kitchen. You're at home there, confident."

"I've cooked my whole life. My grandmother used to teach me how to bake cakes and cookies when I was a child, and my parents worked long hours, so I was the one who prepared the meals most nights." I shrug. "I guess it's just ingrained in my soul."

"You should do it then."

I chew the corner of my lip, offering a small smile. "That's actually one of the reasons I wanted to do this." Covering my face with my hands, I peer out through my fingers. "I've been thinking about it a lot lately, and I thought if I came here, to a real bakery, and dipped my toes in, maybe I'd know for sure."

"And? Do you know?"

I nod. "I do. I do want this, Dallas. And I have you to thank, really. Well, you and Tui."

"Me? What did I do?"

"You opened my eyes and brought me out of my shell. You made me realise I'd given up on my dreams. I'd resigned to the fact I was never going to amount to anything special and that this was my lot in life." I shrug. "But I don't want that to be my lot. I want more from life. I want this." I wave my hands around the homely shop and inhale deeply.

He takes my hand, bringing it to his lips. "Then you should go for it. And I'll do anything I can to help you get there."

"Did I just hear what I think I did?" Tui asks as she places our coffees in front of us. "You're finally going to do it?"

I grin up at her. "I am. I'm going to apply at Petit Patisserie."

"*Anō te pai*! Yes, girl!" Tui drags me out of my seat and throws her arms around me. "I knew you'd find your way back eventually."

"How?"

"Girl, you were made to bake. Even without the formal training, you could have all this if you wanted it. You've always been incredible in the kitchen, which is why," she pulls some papers from her apron pocket, "I printed these out before you arrived." She hands them to me, and I gasp when I see the letter of recommendation with her signature at the bottom. Beneath it are the forms to sign up for Petit Patisserie's night school. "I finally get to repay you for all your help back when I started out." She points to the date at the top. "The next intake is in a few weeks."

"But how did you know?"

She shrugs. "Just a hunch."

Tears well in my eyes as I take in my friend. "I don't know what to say."

"Don't say anything. Just fill in the damn forms already." She grins, handing me a pen.

Chapter twenty-two

The smell of freshly baked bread wafts through the air as we stand by the ovens, waiting patiently for our creations to finish cooking. The completed enrolment forms are in a sealed envelope in my bag, ready for me to post when we leave, and I feel as if a weight has been lifted from my shoulders. I feel free.

"It's good to see you looking so happy, girl." Tui nudges me with her elbow. "I've missed you, and not just in the kitchen."

"I've missed you too." Back when we first met, Tui had been going through a rough break up, and to distract her, I'd taught her how to bake. We'd spent hours in the kitchen coming up with outrageous concoctions and hosting dinner parties with our friends. It's what started her love of cooking, and why I encouraged her to enrol after Ernie had thrown out my acceptance letter and signed me up for what he thought was a better option. I'd been heartbroken, of course, but he'd somehow made me believe I wasn't good enough to make a go of it, and in the end, I'd been grateful to have something to fall back on. It's taken me all this time to realise he was wrong.

"You should come round some time. Meet the kids. Tony would love to see you again."

"I'm sure he would." I snort. Tony had been one of Ernie's best friends. They worked in the same industry and often had 'business meetings' on the golf course.

She places her hand on my arm. "No really, he would. After it came out, what Ernie did to you, Tony washed his hands of him."

"Really?"

"Oh absolutely, girl. A lot of us did actually." She huffs out a breath. "He was an arse, and we could all see it, but I guess no one wanted to rock the boat. Not until it was too late." She takes my hand. "I'm sorry I wasn't a better friend to you."

I turn to her with raised brows. "You were a great friend, Tui. I'm the one who's sorry." I wave my hand out. "Look at what you've accomplished here. I should've been here to celebrate with you, but I was too busy feeling sorry for myself."

"I think we both needed our arses kicked. All these years we've wasted." She shakes her head. "I'm going to be there for you this time though, every step of the way. Hell, I'll give you a job here if you want it."

I chuckle. "Thanks, but I think I need to do this on my own. It's time I took my life back."

"Damn right, girl!" She offers me her fist, and I awkwardly tap mine to it. "But the offer is there if you change your mind. You're always welcome here." She pauses, giving me a sideward glance. "Except for two weeks from now, then you're not." She winks.

"What's happening two weeks from now?" Dallas asks as I groan.

"My birthday."

"Mmhmm. It's a biggun too, eh, girl?" Tui chuckles. "Suz has already been on my case about your cake."

"A big birthday, eh?" Dallas slips his arms around my waist, raising his brows. "How come I don't know about this?"

I tip my head forward, burying my face in his chest. "It's not like I want to shout it from the rooftops. I'm turning… 40." An involuntary shudder runs down my spine. "Told you I was old." Dallas's chest rumbles as he laughs, planting a kiss on the top of my head.

"Is that all? You're in your prime. Wait until you start nearing 50." He shakes his head. "It's all downhill from there." I tilt my head up to see his eyes dancing as he grins.

I slap a hand to his chest with a giggle. "You're not 50."

"No, I'm not. But I am closer to that than I am 40." He purses his lips. "In fact, I think I feel a midlife crisis coming on. Better go buy a Porsche 911 while I can."

"Okay, but only if you don't go trading me in for a younger, flashier model too." I grin up at him.

"I wouldn't dream of it."

"Look at you two, all loved up and googly eyed." Tui sighs. "You better bring him when you visit. He can show Tony a thing or two about wooing a woman."

"I seem to recall a certain someone making you a mixed tape of all your favourite songs back in the day.

And didn't he propose on a flight to Australia like Adam Sandler in your favourite movie?"

Tui sighs again, but this time with a goofy grin on her face. "Yeah, he did."

"Sounds like I need to take lessons from him instead." Dallas pulls out his phone.

"What are you doing?"

"Taking notes on how to woo you." He winks.

"I think you're doing a pretty good job on your own, doc." I push up from the bench and press my lips to his. His hands splay out on my back, pulling me closer to him, and I almost forget we have company. Until she clears her throat beside us.

When we pull apart, Tui is standing there with a grin on her face. "Bread's done. Just in time too. Any hotter in here and you'd start a fire." She fans herself with a tea towel as she makes her way to the oven.

Three round loaves come out, and after tapping each one on the base to check they're ready, she places them on a rack to cool.

"I'll grab you a basket to take them home with you. I'm sure you two have better things to do with your day than sit around here watching bread cool."

"Thanks, Tui. For helping me out today, and for this." I hold up the envelope with my enrolment forms inside. "I really needed this."

"No, you didn't. You already knew you were going to apply. I just gave you a little nudge is all. You've got this."

With dinner in the oven, and our bread cooling on the bench, I get to work on making the apple pie for dessert. I make the sweet pastry from scratch while Dallas watches on with a glass of wine. "You make that look so easy," he says.

"Because it is." I smile, working the dough into the pie tin. "It's my grandmother's recipe, and I've been making it for years. It reminds me of her."

"She sounds like an amazing woman. It's great that she passed on her love of cooking. It's a skill that seems to be declining these days."

"Tell me about it. I bake a lot in the weekends, and with only me here, it doesn't get eaten, so I usually take it in to work. The intern, Daniel, devours about half the tray before anyone else gets a chance. I sometimes wonder if it's the only home cooking he gets." I chop the apples and add them to a saucepan with a dollop of butter, flour, and a little sugar. "He thinks I should set up a stall outside the pubs in the weekends. Reckons I'd make a killing." I grin. "Can you imagine me handing out cupcakes to drunken men on a Saturday evening?"

"It certainly paints quite the picture." He smiles. "But maybe he's got a point. You have to start somewhere, right?"

"I suppose." I pause, flouring the bench again to start on the pie top. "There is something I wanted to run by you."

"What is it?"

"Well, I was thinking about you volunteering with the children, and I wondered if perhaps I could bring some cupcakes or cookies for them on Saturday? I don't know what the protocol is or if it's allowed, but I'd like to do something nice for them and the nurses too." When I look up, he's staring at me with an expression I can't read. "It's a silly idea, isn't it? I don't know what I was thinking."

"Marianne." He reaches out and stills my hand over the rolling pin. "It's a wonderful idea. Let me check with the nurses on the ward and see what we can do. Some will have special requirements."

"Of course. That makes sense."

He places his wine on the bench and cups my chin in his hands. "You are amazing, you know that?"

I roll my eyes. "It's just baking."

"It's not *just* anything. It's a wonderful gesture, and the children will love it, I'm sure." He presses his lips to mine, and all thoughts of finishing the pie fly out the window. I weave my hands up into his hair as I press myself into him. His hands wrap around my back, one sliding up to rest on the nape of my neck, and I melt.

The pot of apples starts to hiss, and I reluctantly pull away. "Just give me one second." I dart over to the oven and pull the pot from the element, tipping the apples into the awaiting pie crust. I quickly roll out the dough and cut a large circle to cover the pie, then using the cutters, I make as many stars as I can. Dallas steps in behind me, his hands on my waist as he watches over my shoulder. I press the lid on the pie and crimp the edges with a floured fork, then brush a little butter on top to help adhere the stars. With Dallas's breath warming my neck, I make quick work of the decoration, eager to get back to what we were doing. I have a feeling I'm going to be getting dessert in more ways than one.

Chapter twenty-three

Setting the pie aside, I turn in Dallas's arms as butterflies swarm in my stomach. I've been wanting this since I first laid eyes on the man, but now that it's a very real possibility, I'm nervous as hell.

His hands trail from around my waist to cup my face, and I swear if my back wasn't up against the bench right now, I'd be a puddle on the floor. My legs are shaking, and I don't know what to do with my hands. It's been so long since I've danced the horizontal cha-cha, and I'm not sure I can remember what to do anymore. But when his forehead presses to mine and our breaths mingle, all my nerves dissipate.

Ever so slowly, Dallas leans in and brushes his lips against mine. He pulls back, his eyes searching mine, and I give a small nod. His lips curl up in the corners, bringing out those crinkles around his eyes, and I'm gone for. I wrap my hands around his neck and pull him to me, taking his lips with an urgency I didn't know I had in me. I guess three years of longing will do that to you.

I break away, trying to catch my breath as I stare into his baby blues. Without a word, I take his hand and lead him up the stairs and to my room.

"Marianne, are you sure? I didn't mean to get carried away. We don't have to do this. I can wait."

I reach for the hem of my shirt, pulling it over my head and throwing it on the floor behind me. "You might be able to wait, but I can't. I feel like I've already waited my whole life for you."

His eyes drop to where my fingers hover over the button of my jeans, and I have to take a breath to steady them. I watch as he reaches for the buttons on his shirt and one by one, he undoes them, exposing his muscular chest to me. There's a dusting of dark curls with a trail leading to the promised land beneath his waistband.

My mouth goes dry, the sight of his bare chest rendering me speechless, and I fumble with my jeans, now desperate to get them off but unable to get the damn things undone. With a groan, I drag my eyes away from him to focus on the task that has me frustrated. God, why won't my hands stop shaking?

Before I even realise what's happening, Dallas is in front of me, his hands resting over mine. "Let me help." His voice is husky and raw, and it sends a flood of warmth straight to my core.

"Thanks," I whisper. "I'm a little nervous. It's been a long time." I bark out a laugh. "But you already know that."

He chuckles, pressing his forehead to mine. "It's been a long time for me too. I don't want to disappoint you."

"Unless you're planning on walking out right now, I don't think there's anything you could do that would disappoint me." I place my hand on his chest, feeling his heart thump beneath my fingers. "I want this, Dallas. I want you."

He closes his eyes, and with nimble fingers, he has my jeans undone in a matter of seconds. He hooks his thumbs through the belt buckles at the side then meets my gaze with a raised brow, as if he needs my permission. Pulling my lip between my teeth, I place my hands on top of his, and we begin the painfully slow procedure of tugging them down my legs. Of all the jeans I own, why did I have to wear the tightest known to man? Sure, they make my butt look great, but they're tighter than a roll of cling film, and I have to lie down and use a coat hanger just to do them up. Of course, if I'd known this was on the cards for tonight, I probably would've chosen differently. Hindsight, and all that.

With the offending pants now pooling around my ankles, I don't dare try to step out of them for fear of tripping. With my track record, I'd end up giving him a black eye, which is really not the kind of sexy I'm going for.

Dallas drops to his knees, one hand slipping behind my knee as he gently lifts and tugs the fabric from my foot before switching to the other side. It's soft and sweet, the way he holds me, but at the same time, extremely erotic.

He stands, letting his eyes rake over my body like a soft caress, and I take the opportunity to do the same. He could easily grace the cover of one of my romance novels. Fabio, eat your heart out.

"Marianne." He says my name with a reverence I've only ever heard in movies and never experienced in real life, and it brings a tear to my eyes. *Great.* Now I'm going to be one of those overly emotional women who cries during sex. I certainly didn't see that coming.

His hands once again cup my cheeks as he presses his lips to each of my eyes and then my mouth, making me forget my train of thought. "You are exquisite."

"And you're…" I rack my brain for an appropriate word to describe him but come up blank. No word does him justice. "You're…"

"It's not like you to be lost for words." He chuckles, nuzzling his nose against mine.

"That's the effect you have on me. For once, I have no words. I mean, look at you." I lean back, letting my eyes drift over the ridges that form his abs. "You could give the statue of David a run for his money, that's for damn sure."

A husky laugh rumbles through his chest as he wraps his arms around me. "I'll take it." His lips find mine as he pulls me close, letting me know just how exquisite he finds me. And judging by the impressive bulge pressing into my stomach, I think it's fair to say he likes what he sees.

I slide my hands down to the front of his jeans, eager to add them to the pile of discarded clothes at our feet. I casually let my fingers brush against him, and I can't help but raise my brows as I pull back. "Forget the statue of David, you put Ron Jeremy to shame with that thing."

He raises an amused brow. "Speaking from experience?"

"Good Lord, no." I shake my head, giggling. "He's not really my type." My eyes widen as I stammer, "I mean, that part is, I guess… I don't find him attractive though. Not that looks matter or anything… I'm sure he's a lovely person, but he doesn't really do it for me…" I trail off, pulling my lip between my teeth. "I don't even think I've seen any of his… films. I've just heard… you know… that it's somewhat impressive."

"Marianne?"

"Mmm?"

"It's okay if you don't find someone attractive. It doesn't make you a bad person."

I cringe, hiding my face against his chest. "Ugh, I'm making this so awkward, I'm sorry."

He tilts my face up to meet his gaze, a grin spreading across his face. "I have no problem with being compared to Ron Jeremy's appendage. It's quite the compliment."

"It is. I mean, that's what I was meaning it to be. God, why am I so bad at this?"

His hands roam down my back to rest on my arse as he leans in and nips at my lips. "I don't know about that. I'm having a great time."

"Well, um, okay then," I stammer between kisses, suddenly not caring so much about the stupid things that keep coming out of my mouth. I give in, moulding my body to his as our hands explore each other, lazily at first, then more frantically as the kiss deepens. My nails claw at his back, needing him closer, and a guttural growl escapes his lips as he pulls back before lifting me and wrapping my legs around his waist. A short few steps has us at the bed, and he lowers me gently, his hands coming up to rest beside my head as he braces himself above me.

He hovers, his eyes searching mine as he pants, and I wrap my hands around his neck, pulling him to me. I need this. I need *him*.

"Please," I whisper against his lips, rocking my hips up to meet his.

His tongue trails down my neck while his thumb hooks the fabric of my bra and tugs. His lips find purchase on my nipple, and I arch my back, pressing myself into him. "Dallas, please."

With one hand still kneading my breast, he plants kisses along my stomach to the top of my panties. I can barely breathe as he laps at the soft skin below. Sliding his hands down my sides, he slowly drags my panties off before running his hands back up my legs in that tantalisingly slow way he did before. Featherlight kisses dot along my inner thighs, and I quiver with a need so strong. I feel as though I could combust with just one touch.

His tongue skates closer to my centre, and I whimper. One flick of his tongue and I'm seeing stars. "Oh God," I cry out, running my hands through his hair and gripping tight. He lets out a groan as his fingers dig into my hips, and I buck against his face, chasing the release I can already feel building. Who knew sex could be so good? I certainly didn't. And when he adds one of those magic fingers to the mix, my eyes roll so far back I can see the pillow behind me. "God, yes, don't stop," I cry out, riding his face like one of those porn stars I always thought were over the top. But I get it now.

The scruff on his face scratches against my thighs as he delves further, and it only heightens the sensation, sending me crashing over the edge. My legs lock around his head as I gasp in breath. "Dallas!"

He wraps his hands around my thighs, slowing his tongue as I come down from my high. I tug at his hair, pulling him up to face me with a sheepish grin on my face. "Well, that was embarrassingly quick. Sorry. I blame those magical doctor fingers of yours."

He chuckles, kissing his way up my body. "You need to stop apologising all the time. I have zero complaints." He holds his hand up, his finger and thumb in the shape of an 'O'.

A blush warms my cheeks as I pull my lip between my teeth. "Well, *I* have one teeny tiny complaint."

His lips pause against my skin. "Oh?"

I pull his face level to mine and rock my hips into his. "You're not inside me," I whisper, claiming his lips.

Chapter twenty-four

I wake with two warm arms wrapped around me and a delicious ache in my body. One I haven't felt in a long time. Susan was right; I *had* been missing out. All those wasted years…

Dallas wraps his arms tighter around my middle, nuzzling his face into the crook of my neck. "Morning." His voice is husky and oh so sexy.

"Morning yourself." I wiggle my hips against him, eager for a repeat of last night even though I know we both have work to get to.

He groans. "You're not making it easy to get up, you know?"

"I think you're doing a pretty good job of that yourself." I chuckle, adding an extra wiggle to my hips before scooting forward. "But you're right. We should get up and ready for—" I let out a squeal as Dallas reaches out and pulls me back into him with a growl. His lips dance along my neck to the sensitive spot just below my ear, and I melt into him. "Okay, maybe just five more minutes."

His hands trail languorously along my curves, his lips brushing ever so gently across my shoulder blades and up my neck, giving me goosebumps. Heat races through my body, pooling at the apex of my thighs as I press myself back into him, urging him on.

One hand slips over my hip, delving to where I need it the most, his thumb tracing circles on my clit and driving me wild.

"Dallas," I whisper, turning my head to capture his lips. His thumb speeds up, and I buck against him, chasing my high. I whimper against his lips, I'm so close already.

"Let go, Marianne," he whispers, holding my gaze. "Let me see you come undone."

He increases his pace, and I can no longer see straight. The man has magic in his fingers. Magic.

I fall so far over the edge of ecstasy, I don't know if I'll ever make it back, and I'm okay with that. "Oh God, oh God, oh God!" My hips buck forward, but Dallas keeps hold of me, slowing his thumb until I'm a puddle in his arms.

He chuckles against my shoulder. "I didn't peg you for the religious type."

"I'm not, but those hands of yours could be their own religion, and I, for one, would happily pray to *that* deity any day of the week." I roll over, throwing my leg over his to straddle him. "I came this close to speaking in tongues." I hold up a finger and thumb. "In fact, I think I can feel a worshipping coming on." I reach over to the bedside drawer and grab a condom, ripping it open and sliding it over his length. His eyes close as his hands find purchase on my hips. Bracing my hands on his chest, I slowly lower myself until we're both gasping for breath.

His fingers dig into my hips as I start a tantalisingly slow pace, hitting my sweet spot with every move, but I need more. Gripping his shoulders, I tug until he's sitting, our chests flush against each other, our breaths mingling as we rock back and forth. His arms wrap around my back, pulling me tight against him as our lips crash together. I no longer know where I end, and he begins. We're two souls joined as one.

"You're so beautiful, Marianne." His whispered words envelope me, caressing me like a warm summer breeze. I clutch at his arms, his shoulders, his back, needing everything he has to give me, and wanting to give him my all in return.

His hands find their way back to my hips, his fingers digging into the soft flesh as he moves with me. I stare into his eyes of blue as he fills me, the steady thrum building to a crescendo as we become more frantic. Our lips collide as we both fall apart, his mouth swallowing my cries, and his arms catching me before I fall.

Our bodies slick with sweat, we rock gently back and forth until our breaths slow enough to speak. Pressing my forehead to his, I peer into his eyes with a grin. "That was like an out-of-body experience. I don't even know who I am anymore."

"You're still the beautiful woman I've come to know and like a lot. Like *a lot* a lot." He winks.

I put on my best tween voice. "Oh em gee, you like, *like* me like me?"

He chuckles, bringing my lips to his. "Yeah, I *like* you like you, Marianne."

I duck my head, peering up at him. "Well good, because I *like* you like you too."
###

"Morning, Marianne," Daniel says as I bustle into the office with a grin on my face. "Someone looks like they had a good weekend."

"I did actually. How about you?" I set down the Tupperware container with the leftover apple pie and throw my jacket over the back of my seat, turning to face him. I'm surprised to find I'm genuinely interested in what he has to say. I *want* to know how his weekend was. I guess over the past few weeks we've formed a strange kind of bond over the whole HookUp palaver.

"Oh, you know, same old, same old. Bit of gaming, few drinks with the lads, met someone from our favourite site." He grins, lifting his coffee cup to his lips. "We're seeing each other again tonight actually." His cheeks colour, and he seems nervous.

I perch on the edge of my desk, wanting to hear more about this girl who has clearly had an effect on him. "Do I detect an actual connection here, Daniel? You like her?"

He looks around the office as if unsure whether to say anything, then he scoots over and sits in my chair, shuffling forward. His excitement to talk about her is endearing, and I feel honoured that he wants to share that with me.

"I do. I like her a lot. Her name is Clara, and she's like no one I've ever met before," he gushes. "She's sweet and funny, and we didn't even hook up that first night, we just sat and talked for hours."

"That's wonderful, Daniel. I'm happy for you. She sounds like a real catch." I smile.

"I think so too." He grins, leaning back in the chair. He nods towards the container. "Is that apple pie?"

"It sure is. I didn't have time to bake this weekend, but this is leftover from our dessert last night. I thought you might like to have it."

"Yeah? You know I do. Everything you make is primo."

"Well, on that note, I have some news of my own." I reach into my bag and pull out the brochure for Petit Patisserie and hand it to him. "I sent away my enrolment for night school."

"Yeah? Shit, Marianne, that's awesome!" He stands, his arms flinging out as if he's about to hug me but not sure if he should. I make the decision for him and open my own arms. It's awkward but sweet.

"Thanks. I don't know if I would've had the courage to try again if it wasn't for you putting the idea in my head."

"Well, I'm glad I could help you out. You'll be running your own bakery in no time." He picks up his container of pie and turns back towards his office. He pauses in the doorway. "I still get to try everything for free though, right?" He grins, waggling his eyebrows.

"I'm sure we can work something out."

"I need wine, stat." Susan flings her bag on the counter, going straight for the open bottle on the bench behind me.

"Bad day?" I ask, lifting the lid off the pot of boiling water and adding a dash of salt before dumping the spaghetti in.

"I work with a pack of imbeciles. But that's not even it." She takes a large gulp of her wine then tops the glass back up to the brim. "My dry spell is over."

"Isn't that a good thing?"

She gives me a wry look. "It should be, yes, but not this way." She shakes her head and shudders. "It was the worst lay of my life, Marianne. Like throwing a hot dog down a hallway bad."

I snort, swallowing quickly before the wine makes its way out my nose. "I'm not sure that means what you think it does."

"Oh, it does." She holds up her pinkie finger. "Couldn't feel a thing. And that's not even the worst of it." She slumps into one of the seats at the counter, resting her head in her hands. "I made the mistake of giving him my number, and now he won't leave me alone." She turns her head in her hands, screwing up her nose. "Reckons I rocked his world."

"Maybe you did."

"Oh, I know I did. There's no doubt about that. I got skills." She throws herself dramatically back on the seat. "That's the problem, you see. I gave him too good of a time, and now he's obsessed with me."

Her phone pings, and she rifles through her bag to retrieve it before swiping the screen. The hint of a smile graces her face.

"That him now?"

Her smile is quickly replaced by a frown as she throws her phone back into her bag. "Ugh, yes." She rolls her eyes, but she can't hide the fact she's enjoying all the attention he's lavishing her with. Susan is great, but she has an overactive appetite for the opposite sex. She likes to play the field and see what's out there, and she's never really settled down or let a man chase her.

"Mmhmm. I can see it's absolute torture for you." I grin, turning back to the stove to stir the meat sauce. If she detects my sarcasm, she doesn't say anything.

"I mean, you know me. I don't go back for seconds, and guys normally appreciate that. But this one…" She pauses, shaking her head. "He's not getting it. Keeps asking me how my day is."

"Oh, the horror. How dare he ask such a thing of you." I smirk, pouring myself another glass of wine.

She flips me the bird, poking her tongue out. "Shut up. You know what I mean."

"I do, but really, what's the harm? So he's a little taken with you. You have to admit, it's a nice feeling, right?"

She trails her finger along the counter, her lips pursed. "I suppose it is kinda nice to feel wanted."

Leaning my elbows on the counter, I level her with a stare. "Was the sex *really* that bad?"

She peeks up at me then closes her eyes. "It was… I don't know… different."

"Good different?"

"I don't know." She shrugs. "Maybe? It was all soft and sweet." She makes a face, and I can't help but laugh.

"So it wasn't hot and sweaty sex like you're used to. That doesn't make it bad."

"Ugh, I guess not, Miss Voice of Reason." She narrows her eyes at me. "Wait a second. What's happening here? Why are you giving me sex advice? This isn't our dynamic." She leans back in her seat, stabbing a finger in my direction. "You had sex, didn't you?"

"I might have." I turn back to the stove, taking the pot of pasta from the element and draining it into the sink. I add a splash of oil and toss it around with the tongs to keep myself busy.

"You naughty little minx! I can't believe you didn't tell me!"

I spin around to face her, leaning my back against the sink. "I'm telling you now, aren't I?" I raise my brow as if to challenge her.

"When, where, and how good was it?" She leans forward, resting her chin on her hands. "I wanna hear *everything*." She waggles her brows.

"Um, last night, upstairs, and amazing," I gush, unable to hide the smile from my face. "We even had a second round this morning. The things he can do to me…" I bite my lip, closing my eyes. "It should be illegal."

"Ooh, that good, huh?" She fans her face, huffing out a breath.

"That good. You were right, I *was* missing out. I had no idea it could be that good." I offer a sly smile.

"Aww, honey." She pushes up from her seat and rounds the counter, taking hold of my shoulders. "I'm so happy for your hooha right now. She deserved a bit of TLC." She drops down to her knees and speaks to my nether regions. "You're welcome."

"You're happy for my hooha? Not for me?"

"Oh—" she waves a hand through the air as she clambers to her feet "—sure, I'm happy for you too, but your coochie needed this after you holding out on her all those years." She shakes her head. "I still can't believe you went three years without."

"Believe me, if I'd known it could be like that, I never would've deprived myself for so long." I sigh wistfully as I switch off the stove and grab some plates.

Susan grabs the cutlery out of the drawer before turning to me with a grin. "Soooo, give me the details. Is he well-hung?"

"Oh God!" I drop my head as I remember the way my tongue ran away with every stupid thought that popped into my head last night.

"Aww, hon, that's okay. Size isn't everything." She rubs a hand up and down my arm.

I turn to her with a raised brow. "Says the woman who complained about a hot dog down a hallway not five minutes ago." I tsk, pointing my tongs at her. "And to answer your question, yes, he's *very* well-endowed." I spoon the meat sauce into the pasta and shake the pot around to coat it. "Definitely no complaints from me." I pause. "I may have let him know that too." I wince, handing her a plate.

"Oh Lord, what did you do?"

"I might've compared him to Ron Jeremy… and then started babbling about how I'm not shallow." I squeeze my eyes tight as Susan just about wets herself laughing. "I was unbelievably awkward. It was so embarrassing." I shake my head, taking a seat. "I'm lucky he thought it was charming."

Susan continues to giggle as she sashays back around the counter to take her seat opposite me before composing herself. "Oh, that was good. I needed that. Haven't had a good laugh in a while." She wipes a finger under each eye.

"I'm glad you find me so amusing."

She looks at me with a sincere expression, reaching her hand across to pat mine. "As your friend, I vow to always find your sex life amusing."

"Gee thanks." I roll my eyes.

She clasps one hand to her chest and flings the other out to her side as she bows slightly. "You're welcome." Digging into her dinner, she points her fork at me. "It can't have been that bad anyway. He stayed over *and* came back for seconds. The man has it bad."

Her words wash over me, sinking in and taking hold of my soul.

Dallas Mahoney has it bad for me.

And I have it bad for him too.

Chapter twenty-six

It's been three days since I've seen Dallas, and even though we're texting every day, it's not enough. I know he's a busy man, but a woman has needs, damn it. Needs that have been dormant for far too long, and now they've been reawakened, I'm like a woman possessed. I can't get him off my mind. I've even taken matters into my own hands once or twice. Just my hands, mind you. I won't be making *that* mistake again.

Still, it's not the same going it solo. Now that I've had a taste of that delectable man, I want more, but I also don't want to come across as needy.

I stare at my silent phone sitting across from me, tapping my fingers against the counter as I contemplate messaging him for a bit of midweek delight.

"Just do it. The worst he can do is say no," I mutter to myself as I swipe my finger across the screen.

Marianne: How has your day been?

Dallas: Well, I had to remove an action figure from someone's backside…

Marianne: Eww, that doesn't sound fun. You seem to be making a habit out of that. New hobby?

Dallas: Could be. Perhaps it's my calling.

Marianne: I couldn't think of anything worse.

Dallas: I imagine it wasn't too fun being the guy it was removed from. I'd say my day was better than his.

Marianne: lol I suppose you have a point there.

Marianne: I don't suppose you feel like grabbing a bite to eat? I understand if you're not up for it after that.

Dallas: I'm always up for anything when it comes to you.

My heart jumps in my chest at the prospect of seeing him again, and I quickly type out a response before he has a chance to change his mind.

Marianne: It's a date then. 7pm?

Dallas: I'll be there with bells on.

Marianne: Damn, I'm gonna have to rethink my whole outfit now. We can't both show up wearing bells.

Dallas: lol see you soon, Marianne.

With my phone still firmly held in my grasp, I do a little happy dance through the kitchen and up the stairs to my room to get ready. I lay out the new lacy underwear I bought on the way home from work, grab a pair of black jeans from the closet and add a fluffy jersey to the pile before jumping into the shower.

Fifteen minutes later, I'm standing in front of the mirror, taming my curls into a messy plait. I moisturise my face and add a dash of lip gloss before grabbing my boots and running back down the stairs. Getting ready is so much faster without all the palaver of fixing my face, and my skin feels great now that it can finally breathe again. I don't know why I didn't do this sooner.

Zipping up my boots, I cock my head as a faint tinkle rings through the air. I check my phone for a notification, but there are none. The tinkle comes again, a little louder this time, and I freeze, trying to pinpoint where it's coming from.

A throat clears from outside my front door followed by another tinkle and a light knock. I swing the door open to find Dallas standing on my doorstep with the tiniest little bell I've ever seen in his hand. He wiggles his hand back and forth with a grin, the bell's itty-bitty chime ringing through the air.

"You weren't joking when you said you'd come with bells on." I laugh, tugging him through the door and planting a kiss on his smug mouth. "I love it."

I love you.

I frown, taken aback by the tiny voice inside my head. It's way too soon for that kind of talk. We've only known each other a few weeks. I can't possibly be in love with him already. Can I?

"I thought you'd get a kick out of it."

"You thought right. Shall we head out?"

He hesitates, pushing his glasses further up on his nose with a sheepish expression. "I was kind of hoping we could stay in tonight." His hand slides around to grip my waist. "I'll still feed you, of course, but..." He sighs, tugging me against him and burying his head in the crook of my neck. "I've missed this, and I don't feel like sharing you with anyone else tonight." His lips dust against my collarbone, and a shiver runs down my spine as I melt into him. "Is that okay?"

Who am I to turn him down?

"It's more than okay. It's what I was hoping for too, I just didn't want to come across all needy." I roll my eyes, flicking a hand through the air as I say it. "Unlike someone else I know." I grin, sliding my hands up to wrap around his neck.

Dallas chuckles, his fingers finding that soft, ticklish spot just below my ribs. My body jerks sideways involuntarily, and I let out a squeal, laughing as I jump back from his roaming hands. "Who's needy?" He lunges forward, his fingers poised for more.

"Okay, okay!" I laugh, holding my hands up in surrender. "You're not needy."

He stops, his fingers still clutching my ribs as he chuckles. "That was far too easy."

"Not needy, just a bit clingy," I say before darting out of his hold and racing up the stairs. Dallas follows, hot on my heels, and once again, I squeal, feeling like a teenager again. It's amazing what a little bit of vitamin D in your diet can do.

Chapter twenty-seven

"You know, I'm going to develop a complex if you keep fobbing me off for the hot doctor," Susan says as she throws her bag on the counter and flops down on one of the stools. She points an accusing finger in my direction. "Weekends used to be my domain."

"First of all, it was one weekend. And last I checked, it's Friday night. Is that not the weekend?" I raise a brow at her while pouring us both a glass of wine.

She huffs out a breath. "Yes."

"And didn't I watch porn with you just the other weekend?"

She rolls her eyes. "For the last time, it wasn't porn. It was some quality cinematic lovemaking." She lifts her glass to her lips, taking a large mouthful before meeting my eyes. I crack first, unable to hold in my laughter. She only just manages to swallow her mouthful before a laugh forces out between her pursed lips. "You can't tell me you haven't gone back and watched it again though, can you?" She quirks a brow with a knowing grin on her face. And she's not wrong.

"I'm pleading the fifth."

"Ha! I knew it!" She takes another mouthful before pushing off her chair and heading for the fridge. "Have you watched it with the doc?" She peers over her shoulder at me, waggling her brows.

I shrug, topping up my glass with a smirk. "We don't really need any extra stimulant."

"Ooh, it's like that, is it? Tell me more." She turns away from the fridge and begins rummaging through my cupboards.

"Can I help you find something?" I ask with an amused expression.

"Where's all the snacks?" She huffs, straightening up. "We always do wine and snacks. It's our thing."

I shrug. "I've been a little preoccupied this week. I haven't had time to bake so much."

"Oh no." She shakes her head. "Nope."

"What?"

"Don't you what me. Just because you're all loved up, doesn't mean you can shirk your responsibilities – namely, feeding me on girls' night." She points a finger at her chest. "I have needs, you know."

"Pretty sure I can't help you with those needs," I say with a snort. "That's what lover boy is for. What's his name again?"

"Gus." She smiles briefly before stabbing a finger at me. "And he's not my lover. Don't change the subject."

I brush past her as I reach into the one cupboard she neglected to check and pull out a bag of Doritos, tossing them at her. "There, now you have snacks."

She stares at the bag of corn chips as if it was a pile of dog turd and not a tasty snack. I huff out a laugh, pulling out the ingredients to whip up some guacamole to hopefully satisfy her cravings. Just the notion of my preparing her something seems to set her at ease, and she rips into the bag, dumping the contents into a bowl and pushing it across the counter to sit beside her wine.

"That's more like it."

"You're lucky I love you." I point my knife at her, and she blows me a kiss.

"Right back at ya, babe." She picks up a chip and inspects it. "I thought you'd be all over the baking practise after your foray with Tui the other day. Speaking of that, have you heard anything from that cooking school yet?"

I shake my head, averting my eyes. "Not yet, no." The cut off day for submissions was yesterday, and even though it's only been a day, there's a little part of me that was hoping they'd call me straight away and accept me with open arms. That they'd remember me from all those years ago and welcome me back into the fold. I mean, really, how hard is it to pick up a phone and ease someone's mind? Every day that ticks by, I know I'll worry just that little bit more that I didn't make the cut. That I wasn't good enough this time around. Or maybe I was never cut out for it in the first place.

No. I *know* I was good enough back then, and I'll do my damndest to prove I am *still* good enough. It's just, well, patience has never been one of my virtues, and I can't stand the suspense of not knowing.

"What's wrong with them? Can't they see talent when it's standing right in front of them?"

"I love your enthusiasm, but they're hardly going to know I'm talented by looking at a piece of paper." *Even if that's exactly what I was expecting them to do.*

Giving the guacamole one last stir, I slide the bowl towards her, giving her a sly look. "I believe you're the one changing the subject now."

She points a finger at her chest, batting her eyes. "Who? Me?"

"Yes, you. Tell me more about this Gus character. Have you seen him again?"

A blush colours her cheeks, and it warms my heart to see her this way. She's always been a one and done type of girl, never wanting to settle down. The fact she's still been in touch with him after a week is telling. She's caught the feelings.

"We met for coffee last night," she admits with a soft smile as she lazily stirs a chip around the guacamole bowl. "I mean, I could hardly turn the guy down when he's been messaging me every day." She rolls her eyes, but her lips and tone betray her. She's got it bad.

"And? How did it go?"

"Oh, you know." She waves a hand through the air, dropping guacamole on the counter as she does so. "Coffee is coffee."

"Sure, but was it *hot* coffee, or lukewarm?"

"Jesus, what's with the third degree, Sherlock? I'm normally the one asking the questions, not the one answering them." She smirks, and I chuckle.

"Annoying, isn't it?"

"*So* annoying."

"And you still didn't answer my question."

"Ugh, fine. The coffee was good. It was… sweet."

I clap my hands with a grin on my face. "I knew it! You like him."

"I most certainly do not."

"Mmhmm. Tell that to your face."

Her hands fly up to probe her cheeks. "I don't know what you're talking about. My face agrees with me. I *don't* like him."

"Sure, sure." I bring my glass to my lips, taking a small sip. "You seeing him again?"

She grins impishly. "Tomorrow night."

"And will he be coming to my birthday? So I can meet the mysterious Gus?"

She purses her lips, scraping a chip around the bowl of guacamole before answering. "He might be. I don't know. I haven't asked him yet."

"Well, make sure you do. It's next weekend, and I want to see who this guy is. Give him the best friend talk, ya know?"

"Oh, I don't think that's necessary. It's not even serious."

"Oh, I think it is. And as your best friend, it's my duty to have the talk with him." She opens her mouth to object, but I quickly hold my hand up, silencing her. "Don't even try to get out of it. I seem to recall a certain someone putting the hard word on Dallas after only one date." I quirk a brow, challenging her to deny it.

"Okay fine." She throws her hands in the air. "You can have the talk with him if you must. But be nice," she warns.

Holding a hand to my chest in mock outrage, I gasp. "I am *always* nice."

"Yeah, yeah." She shifts in her seat, once again going for the wine. "Just, maybe don't try to scare him off." There's a vulnerability in her voice I've never heard before, and I slide into the seat beside her, turning her to face me.

"I would never." I slash my finger in the shape of a cross over my heart.

"Thanks. I just think maybe I might want this one to stick around a bit."

Chapter twenty-eight

With a batch of cupcakes in one hand, and my well-worn copy of Roald Dahl's *Charlie and the Chocolate Factory* in the other, I slide into the front seat and grin at Dallas.

"What have you got there?" he asks as he pulls away from the curb.

I hold up the book that first piqued my interest in creating sweet treats in the kitchen. "*Charlie and the Chocolate Factory.* I adored this book when I was younger. You could say it inspired my culinary skills." I grin. "I thought maybe I could read it to the children."

His smile lights up his entire face as he places his hand on my knee. "That's a wonderful idea. They love a good story."

"My grandmother used to read to me when I'd stay over. We read all of Roald Dahl's books, but this was my favourite. They're some of my most treasured memories; listening to her read." I smile wistfully, taken back to my childhood days when I'd make a small supper of ice cream with shaved chocolate or a sandwich with cinnamon and sugar, then I'd curl up in bed and eat while she read a chapter or two. There was something so magical and calming about it, even with the sugar overload. It was about the same time she started teaching me how to bake. I'd spend hours watching her measure and weigh ingredients, sifting and folding mixtures, making up recipes as she went.

"Sounds wonderful."

"It really was. She's the reason I love to read *and* bake."

"Speaking of baking." He nods to the Tupperware container on my lap. "What's in there?"

I look down at the rows of colourful cupcakes I'd whipped up after Susan left last night. "I made cupcakes for the children. And underneath is another row for the nurses too." It'd taken me several batches before I was happy with the mix. Meeting the strict requirements wasn't easy, but I wanted to do this for the children, and considering they have very little sugar in them, they taste surprisingly good. Not like cardboard as I was expecting. It may even be something I continue playing with for when I do eventually open my own patisserie.

"You came up with something already?" He turns to me with raised brows. "I only gave you the details the other day."

"I know, but I didn't want to show up empty-handed. I stayed up trialling recipes last night." I give him a smile. "It was fun having something to work on."

"I can see that." He grins. "You know they don't expect you to show up with gifts though, right? They're just happy to have you there. Someone different to talk to or listen to. You're the gift all on your own."

"I know they don't expect it. I wanted to do it. It's the least I could do." I turn to look out the window. "We have so much, you know?"

He takes my hand, bringing it to his lips. "I know."

"And I feel like I leave with new knowledge every time. Like these kids teach me things about myself I should've learned a long time ago."

He chuckles, nodding his head. "I feel the same way, and I've been coming a long time. They open our eyes to the world we choose to ignore."

"Yes! How did they get to be so much smarter than us?"

"I think they just look at the world through eyes not tarnished by hatred or guilt or greed." He shrugs. "Society as a whole could learn a lot by looking at the world through the eyes of a child."

Angling my body towards him, I study his face. "Is that why you do it? To see the world as a better place?"

His lips press into a thin line as he gently squeezes my hand. "Yeah, I think it is. It's what I needed after Clarissa… to see the world through their eyes and not through my grief-stricken ones."

I nod. It makes sense. I think anyone in his shoes would've struggled to keep getting out of bed each day. I know I would've. So to make the decision to step out and find a way to make the world less daunting, less of a nightmare, and to help others while doing so, makes him all the more amazing in my eyes.

"I think it's really brave of you to make that choice. To keep striving to find the good when you have every right to see only the bad."

He shakes his head. "I don't see it as a choice I made. It was just something I felt I needed to do."

"You still miss her?" I ask softly.

He nods. "I do. But when I think of her now, it's not with sadness. I cherish the days I was able to share with her." He links his fingers through mine. "I know she'd want me to be happy, to move on." He glances out the side of his eye. "She would've loved you."

I smile at that. "Well of course. Everyone loves me." I bite my tongue with a grin.

"Yeah, they do," he says softly as he brings my hand to his lips once more.

Did he just say what I think he did?

Chapter twenty-nine

Stretching out across his couch, I make myself at home while Dallas changes out of his clown costume. I haven't been able to stop thinking about what he said and whether it means something or I'm reading too much into it. My feelings for him have snowballed exponentially over the last week or so, but that doesn't mean he feels the same way. It *has* only been a few weeks that we've known each other.

But those few weeks have been more real than anything I ever experienced with Ernie. Real enough to know I don't want to lose him. I *want* this man in my life. For better or for worse, he's my end game. I just know it.

I can't tell him that though, he'll think I'm a mental case. No one professes their love after only a few weeks, at least not anyone I know. No, I must've misinterpreted what he meant. There's no way he was saying what I want to believe he was saying. No. Way.

Unless...

Unless he's just as far gone as I am. Perhaps he too has fallen down the rabbit hole of feelings.

Don't be daft. He's a smart man, a thinker. He's not an emotional wreck like me.

God, why am I fighting with myself over this? The only person who knows what he's thinking is Dallas, and when he's ready to tell me, he will. No amount of internal arguing is going to change that.

"You look deep in thought," he says as joins me on the couch, lifting my feet and placing them on his lap. His fingers begin kneading the tender flesh, and I let my head fall back against the arm of the couch, letting out a sigh. "What's on your mind?"

I snort, covering my face with my hands. "Trust me, you don't want to know."

"I wouldn't ask if I didn't want to know." I peek through my fingers to see him smiling at me. "What is it?"

"I really don't think I should. You'll think I'm crazy. It's far too soon."

"Too soon for me to see you're crazy?" he jokes. "I think we're past the point of no return on that one." He slides his hand up my leg to rest on my knee. "I've told you before, I like you just the way you are. Life is always interesting when you're around."

"Yeah, but this is…" I roll my eyes. "Next level crazy."

"Well you have to tell me now. I can't stand the suspense." He drags my hand from my face. "I promise, I won't feel any differently about you."

"That's what I'm afraid of," I mutter under my breath.

"You think my feelings have changed?"

"No, I…" I huff out a sigh. *What the hell, right?* "You said earlier that everyone loves me, and I know it was just a passing comment and didn't mean anything, but I've been thinking about it all day. I know it's crazy to expect you to love me already—"

"*This* is what's been on your mind? If I love you?" He grins, leaning back against the couch.

I cringe, hiding my face again. "It's stupid, I know."

He pulls my hand from my face, tugging me until I'm sitting up. "It's not stupid. Not at all."

"It's not?" I whisper.

"No, it's not." He pauses, tilting his head, his eyes seeking mine. "Because I *do* love you."

My eyes widen. "You do?"

"I do."

"You don't think it's too early to feel that way?"

He chuckles. "No, I don't. If life has taught me anything, it's that you need to embrace the good while you have it, and you, Marianne, are most definitely the best thing in my life right now."

"I am?"

He kisses the tip of my nose. "You are."

I search his eyes, and a slow smile spreads across my face. "You're the best thing in my life too... And I love you too." Cupping his face, I pull him to me, kissing him. "Even if you are a little crazy."

He pulls back, pointing at his chest. "Oh, I'm crazy now too?"

I nod emphatically. "Oh yeah. Bonkers. Crazier than me even. I mean, I was already a lost cause, but you're meant to be a man of science." I grin, pulling my lip in between my teeth. "What kind of doctor falls in love in a matter of weeks?"

"The kind of doctor who knows what he wants when he sees it." He pulls me onto his lap, brushing his lips against mine. "And what I want is you."

"Well, who am I to stand in the way of what you want, doc?" Wrapping my arms around his neck, I lift myself until I'm straddling his thighs. His hands fall to my waist, pulling me into him. I press my lips to his, rocking my hips back and forth in a tantalisingly slow rhythm.

Dallas slides his hands up my back to caress my neck, and tingles race down my spine. I can't get enough of this man. He's everything I always wanted to find but never thought possible.

Threading my fingers through the hair at the base of his neck, I pull him to me. Our lips clash together as I cling to him, needing every inch of him on me. I trail my hands down his back, gathering the hem of his top and tugging until his chest is bare and exposed to me. My top quickly follows suit, landing on the floor behind us. His lips find purchase on my neck, his strong hands holding me away from him as he kisses a trail down to my breasts. He tugs the lacy fabric down, exposing my nipple. His tongue circles my sensitive bud as I arch my back into his touch, and a groan slips from his lips. It's the sexiest sound I've ever heard, and I can't help but whimper in return.

My hips grind down against him, faster, harder, seeking the release I so desperately need. His nimble fingers unhook my bra, and I wrap my hands firmly around his neck so he can touch me.

"Dallas," I murmur between kisses. "I'm so close."

He brings his hands to my waist, his fingers digging into my soft flesh as he pulls me into him. Lights dance before my eyes as I reach a crescendo I've only ever known with Dallas, and I throw my head back, crying out with pleasure as my body seizes. His hands take over, guiding my hips to ride it out as his lips claim mine, devouring my moans.

"I love you, Marianne," he whispers against my lips.

"I love you too, doc."

Chapter thirty

"Try a nine there." Dallas points to one of the blank squares of my sudoku puzzle as he skirts around me to take a seat. I slide his coffee towards him then turn back to my puzzle, tapping my pencil against my chin. He's right, of course.

"What did you want to do today?" I ask, my eyes flicking around the squares on the page. Dallas drags the paper to sit between us, his elbow resting on the counter as he scans the puzzle with me. It's been somewhat of a ritual of mine every morning over breakfast for the past three years.

He points out another square. "Seven."

Oh, he's good.

"How do you do that so quickly?" I ask. "I have a whole ritual I have to do on each box to work out the numbers, and you come along and just know instantly what goes where." I nudge his arm with mine. "Are you some sort of mathematical savant or something?"

He chuckles, taking a sip of his coffee and pushing the paper back in front of me. "Not a savant, just someone who's done his fair share of sudoku." He leans back in his seat. "We would have puzzles on the common room board in med school and it became a bit of a competition to see who could solve them the fastest." He shrugs. "You're looking at the fastest puzzler who ever graced the Otago halls." He holds his hands in the air like an old-timey gunslinger and blows across his fingers.

Giggling, I fold the paper up and push it aside. "I bet that got all the girls chasing you."

"You'd think that, wouldn't you?"

I gasp playfully. "You mean, the sudoku king *wasn't* the big stud on campus? Who'd have thought?"

"You mean to tell me you're not impressed by my skills?"

"Oh, I'm impressed." I push up from my seat and move to stand behind him. Bending down, I whisper in his ear, "I'm just not sure it's enough to get in my pants."

He ducks his head, chuckling. "Pretty sure I already did that this morning." He peeks over his shoulder at me. "Or was that some other stunning redhead in my bed?"

"Better bloody not be any other redhead in your bed," I mutter, taking his face in my hands and pushing his cheeks in until his lips pucker. "I don't like to share."

With my hands still holding his face, he attempts to grin at me. "You're cute when you're fired up, you know that?" I roll my eyes, and he wraps his arms around me, pressing his forehead to mine. "I can assure you, there's no other redhead." He kisses the tip of my nose. "You're more than enough for me."

"Well, good." I slide my hands up his chest to wrap around his neck. "And, for the record, there's no other silver fox for me either."

Those crinkles beside his eyes make an appearance as he beams back at me. "I should hope not. You did profess your undying love for me last night."

"I don't know that I used those words."

He waves a hand through the air. "I'm paraphrasing. The point is, you love me." He grins, giving my waist a squeeze.

"I believe the feeling was mutual."

He nods. "Very much so, which is why I need to ask you a very important question."

"Oh?"

"You see, there's a special day coming up—"

"Ugh, don't remind me." I huff out a breath, running a hand through my curls as I tip my head backwards. "I've only got a few days left in my thirties. A few days left before I'm officially over the hill. Let me enjoy them without the reminders of my impending doom."

He laughs, cupping my face in his palms and pulling me back to him. "It really isn't the end of the world, you know."

"I know, it's just… it's a whole new age bracket! When I fill in forms, I'm no longer in the 25-39 gap. And I liked that gap!"

His laughter rumbles in his chest. "That's what you're worried about? Having to mark a different age bracket on forms?"

"It's silly, I know, but I've been in that age bracket for a long time, it's comforting. I don't want a new one."

"Well," he says, brushing a strand of hair behind my ear, "I've been in that gap for a few years now, and I can assure you, it's not all that bad in there."

"That's easy for you to say, you're a man."

He chuckles. "I don't see what that has to do with it."

"Men don't age the same as us. You get to be silver foxes while we become haggard. And your skin seems to hold its shape for longer while we get lumped with wrinkles."

"There's nothing wrong with wrinkles. They show you've lived. And you certainly don't look haggard by any stretch of the imagination."

I roll my eyes, snorting. "You're just saying that because you want to keep having sex."

He growls, bringing his palms up to cup my face again. "You can be the most frustrating female sometimes, you know that? When are you going to realise I'm head over heels in love with you?" He pulls me into him, holding me tight. "Yes, the sex is great and I'd really like to keep doing that, but if you decided you wanted to be celibate tomorrow, I'd still be here telling you how beautiful you are." He leans back, searching my eyes. "I adore you, Marianne."

My heart swells, and it feels as though it may take over every inch of my body. There's a stupid grin on my face as I stare up into his eyes of blue, and I swear I can hear harps playing or a choir singing somewhere. It wouldn't even surprise me if angels flew down from the sky this very second and proved my disbelief wrong. I could believe just about anything right now, while he's looking at me as if I hung the moon.

I can't wipe this goofy grin off my face, even though it's been far too long to be socially acceptable, but I can't find the words to express how I feel. How does he keep doing that to me? Rendering me speechless?

Staring into eyes that are quickly becoming my favourite colour, I say the only thing I can think of. "Well, someone's getting lucky tonight."

Smooth.

He chuckles. "Okay, but first, can we go shopping?"

I shake my head. "I'm sorry, did you just ask me to go shopping with you?" He nods, grinning. I place the back of my hand to his forehead. "Are you feeling okay?"

"More than okay."

"Really?" I fold my arms across my chest, pursing my lips. "Because I just offered you sex, and you asked to go shopping." I gasp, holding a hand to my mouth. "You're not secretly gay, are you? I'm not your beard, am I?"

He barks out a laugh before cupping my arse in his hands. "I promise, I am not gay. In fact, I'm a little offended you'd think that after this morning." He raises a brow. "Was it not to your satisfaction? Because I seem to recall you taking the Lord's name in vain over and over again." He grins.

My cheeks redden as I recall the things he did to me, and just the thought sends a tingle through my veins. "Oh, that was more than satisfactory." I bite my lip. "*Very much so.*"

A slow smile stretches across his face. "Glad to hear it."

I reach my hands up to wrap around his neck. "In fact, I wouldn't say no to a repeat performance."

His eyes darken as he gives my arse a squeeze. "I'm more than happy to accommodate. But first—"

"—shopping," I finish for him with a roll of my eyes. "I've never known a man to pass up sex for shopping."

"No one said anything about passing it up, just postponing it." His hands slide to my waist. "I want to take you shopping and lavish you with gifts for your birthday."

"You don't have to do that."

"I know I don't. I want to, and I won't take no for an answer."

Chapter thirty-one

Skipping around Kitchen Emporium like a kid let loose in a candy shop, I make a mental list of all the pretty new appliances I'll need to kick off my dream. There are shelves upon shelves of KitchenAid mixers in every colour of the rainbow, with all the matching accessories, and I feel like I've died and gone to heaven.

"Something tickle your fancy?" Dallas asks as he comes up behind me.

I spin to face him with a grin splitting my face. "Where do I even begin?" I wave my hand at the shelves. "These are top of the line. All the best chefs have them." I count on my fingers. "Jamie Oliver, Gordon Ramsey, Nigella…" Turning on my heel, I inhale as I take in the range of mixers on display. "I've always wanted to own one, but the $900 price tag has put me off," I say sheepishly.

"Who can put a price on dreams though, right?" Dallas places his hands on my shoulders, leaning in to whisper in my ear. "You should buy one. Treat yourself. It's your birthday."

I dig my toe into the floor, twisting my foot around as I tap a finger to my chin, my lips pursed. "I don't know. The price…"

"Then let me buy it for you. Which one do you want?" He pulls his wallet out from his back pocket, and I quickly gather his hands in mine, shaking my head.

"No! It's far too expensive."

"Not when I know it'll be put to good use. Plus, it'll be nice to know I had a hand in you becoming a world-renowned pastry chef by buying your first mixer."

"I couldn't possibly accept it."

He drops his hands, sighing. "At least let me pay half. You only turn 40 once."

"You *do* only turn 40 once…" I peek over my shoulder, my eyes falling to the bright red mixer in the centre. It has a sheen to it that makes me think of Christmas. "I *have* always wanted one."

"Go on, live a little."

I can't contain my grin as I rock back and forth on my heels. *Am I really going to do this?*

Yes. Yes, I am.

My heart races as I make my way to the counter. The cashier looks up as I approach, a fake smile plastered across her face. "Can I help you?" she asks in a bored tone.

"Um, yes, please. I would like to purchase one of your mixers." I point across the room, as if she hadn't been eyeballing me the entire half hour I'd been standing there.

The cashier's eyes follow my hand, and she straightens, a real smile gracing her face as she clears her throat, and I can practically see the dollar signs shining in her eyes. "Oh, yes, of course. Which one would you like?" She skirts around the counter, rushing to the display and holding her hand out like a gameshow assistant.

"The red one in the middle."

"Excellent choice," she gushes, clicking her finger at one of the assistants floating about. "Candy-red KitchenAid please." The assistant nods and darts through a door at the back. The cashier turns her attention back to me. "Anything else to go with it?" She waves her hand at the wall of accessories. "Slicer and shredder? Juicer? Ravioli roller? Mincer?"

I shake my head, though my heart is screaming for me to buy all the things. "Just the mixer for today, thanks." I follow her to the counter to pay, feeling as though I'm in a dream. Dallas pulls out his card and hands it over, and I do the same.

The assistant returns from out the back, carrying a large box with the bright red mixer on the front and places it on the counter with a flourish. The cashier finalises the sale then slides my mixer into a carry bag. My heart skips a beat. This right here marks the moment I take a step towards my future. The moment I invest in myself.

Dallas takes the carry bag in one hand and guides me through the door with the other. "How does it feel?"

"Like I can't stop smiling," I say with a giggle. "I can't believe I just did that. I can't believe *you* just did that." I reach up on tiptoes to kiss his cheek. "Thank you."

"It's my pleasure. Just don't forget me when you become the next *Naked Chef*." He winks, and I snort back a laugh.

"Trust me, there's no way you'll be seeing my bare backside in a kitchen on TV."

"How about in a kitchen in my house?" he wagers.

Pulling my lip between my teeth, I stare up at him with hooded eyes. "Now *that* I can manage. I mean, you *did* just buy me half a mixer. But I do have one condition—" I waggle my eyebrows, "—if I'm getting naked, so are you."

His eyes drink me in as he licks his lips, leaning forward. "Was there ever any doubt?"

Chapter thirty-two

Wearing nothing but an apron and the smile on my face, I dance around the kitchen to the sound of my new mixer whisking egg whites to perfection. As promised, I promptly stripped out of my clothes the second we walked through the door, leaving a trail of garments to the kitchen. Dallas had followed behind, adding his clothes to the piles, until he too was naked but for a pinny tied around his waist.

I gradually add in the caster sugar followed by the mix of cornflour, vanilla, and vinegar then leave it to work its magic.

Moving to stand in front of the fridge, I'm suddenly distracted by visions of the oh-so-sexy food play scene in *9 ½ Weeks* playing through my head, and I can't help but wonder if Dallas would be up for that. Then I giggle as I recall my conversation with Susan not so long ago.

Even the most vanilla of men would be turned on knowing you had something kinky up your sleeves.

Well, I'm not wearing any sleeves, but I can certainly pull something kinky out of the fridge. I spy a bottle of whipping cream in the back. "That'll do the trick," I mutter to myself as I grab it and unscrew the lid. Closing the fridge door, I spin on my heels to see Dallas leaning against the counter, a satisfied smirk on his face.

With as sexy a walk as I can muster while he's watching me, I make my way over to him, running a hand up his chest. "Thank you," I whisper, setting the cream on the counter.

"What for?"

"Convincing me to buy this." I wave my hand at the mixer without taking my eyes from his. "I would've kept pining for it but never actually doing anything about it otherwise."

He takes hold of my hips, pulling me into him. A jolt of pleasure fizzes through my veins, settling in the apex of my thighs. "Same way you were pining over me?" His lips stretch into a cheeky grin.

I quirk a brow. "Wasn't it the other way around?"

He chuckles, shaking his head. "I did go after you, if you recall. And you literally fell head over heels for me."

I laugh, remembering that fateful moment when I lost my balance after he called my name. That moment that very nearly didn't happen because we were both too scared to go after what we wanted.

Well, no more. That Marianne has left the building, and a new and improved Marianne has taken to the stage.

Reaching around him, I flick the switch to stop the blades from turning. "Let me just check this real quick." I push up the head of the machine and unhook the bowl, then with a smirk, I quickly raise the bowl and tip it above his head.

"Hey!" He ducks out of the way, laughing. "What are you doing?"

"What? You never heard how to tell if you've whipped egg whites enough?" I grin mischievously. "All the best chefs do it."

"Oh really?" He folds his arms across his chest, leaning back against the counter.

Swinging the bowl back to an upright position, I swipe two fingers through the mix and hold them in the air. "Mmhmm." With a flick of my wrist, I send the sweet-smelling mix flying through the air to land on his cheek. I suck my lips in to stop from laughing as I go in for another swipe. "Looks ready to me." I flick again, and Dallas shakes his head, his lips twisted up into a half-grin.

"Two can play at that game." Before I can stop him, he grabs the bowl from my hands and scoops out a handful, smearing it down my neck and chest.

"Oh, it's like that, is it?" I lunge for the bowl, but he holds it above his head. Standing on tiptoes, I press up against him, rubbing meringue all over him. Our eyes meet, and for a brief second, we just stare at each other with amusement. And then I remember that we're both naked and now covered in food.

Damn. Kim Basinger, eat your heart out.

Bracing my hands on his shoulders, I lean into him, running my tongue along his cheek to lap up the meringue. He inhales sharply, and the arm holding the bowl lowers. With his thumb, he gathers a dollop of the fluffy white cloud and runs it gingerly across my top lip. A whimper escapes me as he lowers his mouth to mine. In an achingly slow fashion, he runs his tongue along my lip, stealing my breath as he does. It's the single most erotic thing I've ever experienced in my life.

His fingers fumble with the ties of my apron, and then I'm standing in front of him, completely bare but for a slather of meringue across my front. Dallas's eyes roam across my body, taking it all in as he removes his own apron and throws it behind him.

Forgetting I'd put the cream on the counter without a lid, I let him lift me, placing me on the cool surface. My bottom nudges the bottle, and it topples over, spinning and pouring cream all over the benchtop and me. I squeal as the thick liquid oozes into places it shouldn't be. My hands wrap around Dallas's neck, and I lift myself off the counter so I'm half in the air and half in his arms, my breasts pressed against his face.

When I look down, all I can see is his nose buried between my breasts and meringue hanging from his forehead. I can't stop the giggle that bursts from my mouth as I slide my way down his body, coating him in even more meringue in the process.

I peer at the carnage behind me. There's cream everywhere. Flowing off the counter onto the floor, dripping into the ceramic sink. Not to mention the icky mess I can feel dribbling down my thighs, and not in a good way.

Holding my hand across my mouth, I make a scratchy walkie-talkie type sound. "Clean up on aisle four."

Dallas grabs my hands, pressing his forehead to mine as he chuckles. "We make quite the mess, don't we?"

I grin, shrugging. "I don't know. It's kinda art nouveau, isn't it?"

"Is it?" he asks, and I erupt into more giggles.

"I have no idea. It sounded good though, right?"

As he leans back, a string of meringue forms between our foreheads, and we both laugh. "Perhaps a shower is in order?"

"I *do* feel particularly *dirty.*"

Dallas growls, enfolding me in his arms and lifting me until my legs wrap around his middle. His hard length presses against me, and I let out a soft moan as I position myself over him, rocking my hips as he strides up the stairs towards the bathroom like a man on a mission.

Kicking the door open, he sets me down on the large granite vanity while he adjusts the taps in the shower. Water cascades from a large central shower head, forming something akin to a waterfall, and a small ribbon of light shines against the dark tiles, giving a masculine yet sensual vibe to the space.

Taking my hand, Dallas leads me under the warm water with him. He takes a cloth from the glass wall and gently wipes across my forehead, around my face, and down my neck to my breasts. I arch my back, leaning into him with a sigh as I wrap my arms around his waist.

"So beautiful," he whispers against my ear, eliciting a shiver down my spine. Goosebumps break out over my skin despite the warmth of the shower and

Dallas pressed against me. This man does things to me I never thought possible.

My hands twine through his hair, and I tug, bringing his lips to mine to swallow my moans. His hands slide over my curves, exploring every inch of my body until he's on his knees in front of me. Looking up at me, he takes my leg and guides it over his shoulder before running the tip of his finger through my folds. That touch alone sends a shudder through me, and I can't help but rock my hips, urging him on.

His hands wrap around to cup my behind as he positions his mouth over my sensitive nub, sucking gently at first, then with more fervour as I try to buck against him. I brace my hands between the tile and the glass wall, tipping my head back as I ride his face to oblivion.

When he comes up for air, I'm left panting, my head bowed down to my chest as I catch my breath. "I should get dirty with you more often."

He chuckles as he gets to his feet, rubbing a hand down over his mouth and chin. I bring his lips to mine in a crushing kiss, tasting myself on his tongue. With my hands on his chest, I push him against the wall with a smirk. "Your turn."

I run my tongue down his chest and abs, my hands following over the firm ridges. On my knees, I peer up at him as I take his length in my hands and pump from root to tip, slow and firm. He lets out a growl, his hand fisting in my hair. With my hand still wrapped firmly around him, I lick around the tip before enveloping him in my mouth. His eyes close briefly before locking with mine as I bob back and forth, my hand working in tandem to bring him to release.

"Oh Jesus, Marianne," he hisses between his teeth. His hand tightens in my hair, and I can tell he's holding back. I'm not having that. I quicken my hand, swirling my tongue around his tip with every lap. When I moan against him, his fist clenches and his head falls back against the wall.

"Jesus Christ." His hand slaps against the tile behind him as his hips jerk forward and hot spurts flow down my throat.

I pull back with a satisfied smirk, dabbing at the corners of my mouth with my thumb. "Who knew getting dirty could be so fun?"

Chapter thirty-three

Closing down my computer, I take another quick glance at the unopened email sitting on my phone.

Petit Patisserie Night School Registrations.

It arrived a little after lunch and has been haunting me ever since. I have so much riding on this, and yet, I can't bring myself to open the damn thing.

There's only one other person who knows how this feels, and right now, I need her by my side. Throwing my things into the car, I fire off a quick message.

Marianne: You still at work?

Tui: Doors are closed, but I'm still here. Come out the back.

Marianne: Thanks. See you soon.

I tuck my phone in my bag; out of sight, out of mind, or so they say. But the damn subject line is engraved on my brain, and I see it every time I close my eyes. *Petit Patisserie Night School Registrations.*

What if I didn't get in? What will I do then? There are other schools, but none as prestigious as Petit Patisserie. That place was my dream school way back when, and it still is now. I don't want to go anywhere else.

Pulling out of the carpark, I make my way to Tui's bakery and park out front. I grab my bag and head down the side alley to the back door where Tui stands waiting. "*Kia ora.* You all set for the party on Friday?" She ushers me inside, closing the door behind us.

"As ready as I can be. With Suz organising it, anything could happen."

Tui chuckles, nodding. "You're not wrong there, girl." She leads me through to the front, pulling out a chair at the counter. "Coffee? Machine's still on. You caught me before I finished shutting everything down."

"Mmm, thanks, coffee would be great."

While Tui makes the drinks, I pull my phone from my bag, bringing up the email and staring at it until the screen goes black. My hands are sweaty, and my throat is dry. I can't recall a time I was this nervous aside from that first date with Dallas before I knew it was him. And that turned out pretty damn good, so maybe I'm worrying about nothing.

Tui places a frothy cappuccino in front of me with a *koru* drawn in the foam. "Why do you look as though you're going to be sick?" She folds her arms across her chest. "Everything okay?" Her eyes narrow. "That man of yours hasn't done something, has he?"

I wave my hand through the air dismissively. "No, no, nothing like that." I swallow the lump in my throat, pushing my phone towards her. "I got the email today," I whisper.

"Email?"

"From Petit Patisserie."

Tui's face lights up. "Ooh, girl, that's exciting! Why you look so sad then? It's a time to celebrate!"

"I haven't opened it yet. I don't even know if I got accepted."

"Well, shoot, girl. Why the hell not?"

I meet her gaze. "I'm too scared to open it. I want this so much, Tui. More than I even realised." Pulling my lip between my teeth, I run a finger along the rim of my cup. "I don't know what I'll do if I don't get in."

"No point worrying when you could just open the email and see for yourself. Come on, I'm right here for you, no matter what the outcome." She nudges the phone back towards me. With my breath held, I open the email and instantly deflate.

"We regret to inform you…" Tears well in my eyes before I can go any further.

"Aww, honey." Tui comes around and pulls me into her arms. "There'll be another intake in a few months. You just need to keep on applying until they accept you."

I nod against her chest. "Yeah, I guess."

"Or," she pulls back and tucks a stray hair behind my ear, "if this is really what you want to do—"

"It is. More than anything."

"Then why don't you bite the bullet and apply for the full-time course? It'll take you half the time it would by going to night school, and I can offer you an apprenticeship here for extra credit."

"I don't know, Tui. I have the mortgage to pay…"

"But this is your dream. And you can't put a price on dreams. You've got a few months to work something out with your bank, and I'll do what I can on my end. I can't pay the big bucks, but I can do more than minimum wage for you." She wraps her hands around my shoulders. "Come on, Marianne. We can make it work. You deserve this. It's your time now."

Her eyes shine with so much hope and promise, and it's contagious. My mind's already whirling with ideas on how I could make this work. Between the savings I have in the bank and taking on the apprenticeship, I think I could maybe manage to swing it. All I have to do is quit my secure job of five years and go back to school full-time. Sure, money will be tight for a while, but I can afford to go without a few things for a while. It's only two years, after all. A small price to pay to follow my dream.

I look at Tui with a grin. I knew there was a reason I needed to be with her today.

"*Auē,* you're going to do it?"

I nod, pushing up from the chair and bringing her in for a hug. "I am. I'm going to do it."

Chapter thirty-four

"Can I borrow that platter thing you have? You know the one, it's red or something, about yea big." Susan draws an odd shape in the air as she rushes through the door. "And if you've got some bags of chips I can grab, that'd be great too. Maybe some of that guacamole." She begins opening drawers and fishing about. "Didn't you have balloons in here?"

"No hello? No happy birthday?"

Susan gives me a look that could level the strongest of men. I hold my hands in the air, palms out. "Okay, okay. Third drawer down. There should be chips in the cupboard up there, I can whip up some guacamole in a sec, and is this—" I drag a large oval platter from my cupboard, holding it up, "—the one you're looking for?"

"Yes! Thanks!" She snatches it out of my hands, gathering up the other goodies she's pilfered and throws them in a bag. "Why aren't you dressed yet?"

"Shoot, did I forget to put clothes on again?" I look down at my black jeans and matching t-shirt, holding my arms out to my sides. "Is this like the *Emperor's New Clothes*? Am I the only one who can see what I'm wearing?" I turn to her with wide eyes as I clamp my arms around my body and bend double.

"Smartarse."

"I love you too."

"Seriously though, I know you're going all low maintenance now and not wearing makeup and whatnot, but I wanna at least see you in a dress and heels when you get there. It's your birthday, not a bloody funeral."

"Yes, ma'am."

She sucks in a breath, her hands fisting on her hips. "You did *not* just ma'am me."

I open my mouth to speak just as Dallas knocks on the door and walks in. "Evening, ladies." His arms wrap around my waist from behind, and he kisses the top of my head. "Happy birthday, beautiful."

"Thank you."

"All under control for tonight? Need me to do anything?"

"Yes," Susan pipes up. "You can make sure she's wearing something a little more birthday girl and a little less mourning." She breezes past towards the door. "And don't forget the guacamole. Love you!" Then she's gone just as quickly as she arrived.

"Is she always this bossy?" Dallas chuckles, nuzzling into my neck.

"Susan is many things, and bossy is *definitely* one of those things." I smile, spinning around to face him. "But I wouldn't change a thing about her."

Gripping my shoulders, he holds me at arm's length, twisting his lips to the side. "So, what's wrong with what you're wearing?"

I shrug, rolling my eyes. "Apparently it's not appropriate party attire." I chuckle, rounding the counter to start on the guacamole. "And she's right. I was never going to go in this anyway. I mean, it *is* my birthday after all."

"Which brings me to my next question. Why are *you* the one making guacamole?"

I pause chopping the avocado to look at him. "Well that's easy. Susan is in love."

"I don't follow."

"Susan is *never* in love. She's a one-night stand, booty-call kinda gal. But she's actually found someone she likes, and he's coming to the party tonight." Scooping the avocado into a bowl, I grab a lemon and slice it open. "She's out of her comfort zone with him, and I'm her safe place. I doubt she actually needed any of this stuff but coming here and bossing me around is her way of coping." I shrug as if it's the only logical explanation. "That and I make the best guacamole."

Dallas chuckles, watching me with a smirk. "So you knew she'd be here for something, and you were just messing with her by dressing in black?"

"Oh yeah. If I'm going to be in a room full of people celebrating my age, I'm going to dress it up not down." With a clean cloth in my hand, I wipe down the bench before washing my hands in the sink. "Could you do me a favour and find the lid for that bowl while I go up and get changed?"

"Of course. Sing out if you need a hand up there." He winks, and I can't help but blush. I would like nothing more than for him to give me a hand, but that would inevitably end up with us being late, and Susan would kill me.

"I think I can manage, but I may need a hand getting undressed later." I wink, adding an extra wiggle to my hips as I walk out the door and up the stairs.

Twenty minutes later, and we're in the car and on our way. My hair is twisted up on top of my head, and I've got my new green polka-dot rockabilly dress on, complete with strappy heels. Susan will be proud.

We pull up to the carpark out back and make our way inside. The pub is quiet for a Friday night, but it's still early. In fact, I'll be lucky if Daniel and Clara even show up before the end of the party. Young ones these days don't normally venture out of the house until at least eleven.

Balloons hang by the entrance to the function room, and there's a large sandwich board with "Marianne's 40th" plastered across it in bold writing. As if I need the entire bar knowing how old I am.

When we walk through the door, Susan rushes over, taking the bowl from my hand and adding it to the trestle table laden with food. She's certainly pulled out all the stops.

"Do you think I have enough?" she asks with a harried expression. In all our years together, I've never seen her look so worried before.

"Susan, breathe. It looks great. Thank you."

She meets my eyes and inhales deeply before huffing it out. "Sorry, I don't know what's wrong with me."

I link my arm through hers, dropping my head to her shoulder. "I do, and I think it's great."

"Please, enlighten me. Because I'm a sweaty mess."

"You're in love," I sing-song, much to her chagrin.

"Eww. Blasphemy. I am *not* in love."

"It's sweet that you think that, but you are one hundred percent into this guy."

She frowns, her finger already lifting to make a point. "I… Gus!" Her eyes dance as she looks over my shoulder, and it's as clear as day, even if she's not ready to admit it to herself, she's in love with this guy. She takes my hand and drags me over to meet him. "Gus, this is Marianne and Dallas. Guys, this is Gus."

"Hi, Gus, it's lovely to finally meet you." I offer my hand, which he accepts. His grip is firm, his hands rough and calloused. He has a wiry frame, is a little on the shorter side, with broad shoulders, and when he looks at Susan, his face lights up.

"It's nice to meet you too. And happy birthday." He leans in awkwardly, pecking me on the cheek.

"And what do you do, Gus?" Dallas asks as they shake hands.

"I'm a builder. Mainly commercial stuff."

"Oh yeah? You ever build a bakery?"

"Dallas! It's a bit early for that kind of talk. I haven't even got in yet." I shake my head.

"Not yet, but you will."

"Damn right, she will," Susan adds. I love how much faith they have in me. It makes it that much easier to believe in myself, knowing they have my back every step of the way.

"Happy to help if and when you need me." Gus grins, rocking back on his heels.

"Did somebody order a cake?" A three-tiered cake covered in macarons, cookies, and chocolate comes through the door with Tui staggering beneath it.

"Oh my God, let me help." I rush over and take an edge, helping her manoeuvre it onto the table. Once it's settled, I take a step back and examine it. Everything is made to perfection, right down to the tiny rosebuds fashioned out of fondant that sit atop the macarons. "Tui, this is amazing. It must've taken you hours."

She waves a hand through the air. "It's the least I could do." She pulls me in for a hug, kissing my cheek. "*Rā whānau koa*. The happiest of birthdays to you, girl."

"Thank you."

"You remember Tony?" She hooks a thumb over her shoulder, pointing to her husband wrangling two small children.

"Of course. Tony, how are you?" I smile, offering my hand, which he ignores, instead pulling me in for a hug.

"I just wanted to say how sorry I am for what happened between you and Ernie."

I shake my head, batting a hand through the air. "No need, honestly. It was for the best."

"Ah yes, Tui tells me you've got a new beau."

"I do. Dallas is his name. He's a doctor."

Tony's smile stretches across his face. "That's great, Marianne. I'm happy for you."

"Thanks. I'm in a really good place right now."

"Well good. You deserve it after what he put you through." He frowns, shoving his hands in his pockets. "I only wish I'd seen it earlier."

"Even if you did, I probably wouldn't have heard what you had to say." I reach out and rub a hand down his arm. "Honestly, Tony, it's fine. *I'm* fine."

He looks at me for a moment then nods, seemingly happy with what he sees. A tiny hand reaches up and tugs his shirt, and he scoops up a little brown-haired beauty with big green eyes. She tucks her head into his neck, her wide eyes taking me in as she sucks her thumb.

"And who might you be?" I ask, my heart melting at the sight of her.

"This is Aroha." Tony plants a kiss on the top of her head. "She's two. And this one," he wraps his other hand around the shoulders of an adorable wee boy with matching eyes and a cheeky grin, "is Nikau."

"I'm this many," Nikau pipes up, holding out two fingers and a thumb.

"Wow, three? You're nearly as old as me." I grin, and he giggles, stepping out from behind his father's legs, puffing his chest out.

"Yup." He nods matter-of-factly.

"I see you've met the ratbags," Tui croons as she joins us.

"I have. They're just beautiful, Tui." I meet her gaze, shame spiralling through me at not being there for her. I've missed so much.

"Yeah, we like them, don't we, Tony?" She ruffles Nikau's hair, and he looks up at her adoringly. I've never had much of a maternal bone in my body. I don't mind hanging out with other people's kids, but I can give them back when I'm done. The idea of having my own though, that has never been on the agenda, but seeing these two cherubs is almost enough to make me change my mind.

"Yeah, they're all right I guess," Tony answers with a grin.

"Hey!" Nikau says, pouting.

"You know I love you, sport. Come on, let's go and grab some drinks and let these two catch up." Tony points towards the bar before kissing Tui on the cheek.

I watch him juggle Aroha on his hip while trying to keep up with Nikau as he darts around the tables. "You must have your hands full with those two and the bakery."

"It can be a challenge at times, but Tony's great with them. He took a step down from the firm when the bakery started taking off, and now he runs his own business from home so he can be with the kids."

"Oh wow, that's quite a change from the Tony I used to know."

Tui chuckles. "Isn't it though?"

"It certainly agrees with him. He's like a new man."

"Girl, you have *no* idea." She fans her face with her hand, and I can't help but laugh at the expression on her face. "A change of pace can really do wonders for your libido, let me tell you."

"Ooh, now this sounds like a conversation I wanna get in on." Susan sidles up beside me, linking her arm through mine. "I heard the words pace and libido. Fill me in."

"Oh no you don't." Tui waggles a finger in the air. "You, of all people, don't need to be getting tips from an old married woman." Susan makes to speak, but Tui touches her finger to her lips. "Don't go pretending like you haven't got yourself a little something going on over there." She purses her lips, jutting her hip out. "Who's the new guy?"

Susan blushes, pulling her lips between her teeth. "That's Gus," she gushes.

"Oooh, girl." Tui leans back with a grin. "You really like this one, don't you? I never thought I'd see the day."

"Oh shut up. You make me sound like a horndog."

"Uh, yeah, because you are, or at least, the old Susan was." I duck my head to hide my laughter as Tui continues to wind her up. It makes for a refreshing change. "You're not telling me you've gone and caught the love bug?" She waggles her brows suggestively, and I just about lose it.

"Jesus Christ, you guys. What's with everyone throwing the L word around? It's just a bit of fun."

Tui meets my eyes, and we both nod knowingly. "Mmmhmm, whatever you need to tell yourself, girl."

Chapter thirty-five

"I swear to God, I didn't invite him." Susan peers over her shoulder then pulls me aside with an apologetic look. "I don't know why he's here."

My heart races as I glance over her shoulder to see my ex-husband at the bar with a young bimbo on his arm. Not the same secretary he'd been with the last time I'd laid eyes on him though. No, this is a new one, and that makes me feel things I shouldn't be feeling. I hate that just the sight of him is enough to send me spiralling backwards.

Inadequate.

Not good enough.

Let myself go.

My hand lifts to my undyed hair, smoothing the lose strands back into the twist, as if that will miraculously make it look better.

"Don't go there, Marianne." Susan takes my hand, and my eyes find hers. "You look beautiful. Don't let him rattle you." She peeks over her shoulder, and I can't help but follow her gaze once more. I try to make myself see him for what he is, but too many years of low self-worth is hard to ignore.

"What do you want me to do? Shall I see if I can get him kicked out?"

Yes.

"No." I shake my head. "It's a public place. He has just as much right to be here as we do." I tear my eyes away, willing those old insecurities to take a hike. "We'll just keep to ourselves."

I plaster a fake smile across my face and raise my glass to my lips. My eyes involuntarily find his beady ones once more, and he smirks.

"Marianne?" Dallas takes my hand and steps in front of me, effectively blocking my view and calming my racing heart. "Are you okay? You look pale." He holds the back of his hand to my forehead with a worried expression on his face.

"I'm fine. Just saw a ghost from my past. No big deal."

His jaw tightens as he turns to look behind him, but I palm his cheek and turn him back to me, planting a kiss on his lips.

"Forget him. He's not worth it." And right now, with Dallas by my side, I almost believe myself.

"I'm going to the little girls' room," I announce as I push up from my seat.

"You want me to come with?" Susan asks, a look of concern on her face.

"No, it's fine. You stay here and get us a refill. I won't be long." I smile reassuringly and make my way down the hallway towards the toilets. For once, there's no line, and I'm in and out in mere minutes. I hold the door open for the lady walking my way, then head back down the hall to my friends.

"Well, well, well," an all too familiar voice sneers from behind me, and I feel the hairs on the back of my neck stand at attention instantly. I've made it this far without having to speak to him, and I curse my tiny bladder for putting me in this position.

I turn slowly to see Ernie sauntering towards me, his eyes raking over my body from head to toe. I hate that I feel naked under his gaze, and not in a good way, but I force myself to stand strong and not flinch.

I'm a better person. He has no control over me anymore, I chant to myself.

"I see you've lost some weight. Pity about the rest of you," he sneers, and I can smell the alcohol on his breath. He never was able to hold his liquor well.

He reaches a finger out and strokes down the length of my cheek. "You used to have such a pretty face, but now you just look old and haggard. It's only a matter of time before that man you've been hanging off sees you for what you are and finds himself a younger—" his eyes flick to my breasts "—perkier model."

I know he's wrong. I know he's just trying to hurt me. But there's also a tiny part inside that agrees with him. A tiny part that needs to take a hike.

"You know what though?" His hand drops down to his fly, lowering it as he takes a step closer. "I can look past it just this once. It *is* your birthday after all." He smirks, palming himself as he sucks his teeth in the way that always used to grate my nerves. "Whaddaya say? A quickie, for old time's sake?"

Bile rushes into my mouth at the thought of him touching me, but before I can form words, two hands slip into mine, and Tui and Susan step up beside me.

"Marianne?" Tui glares at Ernie. "Everything okay here?"

"Mmhmm. Everything is fine. Give me a minute?" I meet their eyes, giving both their hands a squeeze. "There's something I need to do."

They search my eyes and seem to find what they're looking for. With a nod, they step back. "We'll just be over here." Susan glares at Ernie, making sure he knows she's got her eyes on him, and I love her for it. Having them here gives me that extra bit of confidence I need.

Stepping forward, I take a good long look at Ernie. If I'm honest, time has not been kind to him, and that gives me a tingle of satisfaction. His hair is thinning and there's a slight paunch to his stomach. Still, he carries himself with that same air of arrogance he always had. An arrogance that seems misplaced the more I look at him.

"I knew you couldn't pass it up." He grabs himself again, and I fight to swallow the bile that threatens once more. "You always were a bit desperate."

I duck my head down, pursing my lips. "You're right, I was. But only because *you* made me believe I wasn't worth the ground you walked on." I take another step towards him, my finger pointed at his chest. "But now, I see you for what you really are. A pathetic excuse for a man who has to make himself feel big by putting others down." I shake my head. "I don't know what I ever saw in you."

He frowns, his eyes raking over me as if he can't believe it's me saying these things. "You and I both know you were gagging for it."

"Oh that's it," Susan says from behind me. "Let me at him."

I hold up a hand, my eyes never leaving his. "Thanks, guys, but he's not worth it." And then I spin on my heels and strut back down the hall, leaving him standing there with his cock in his hand.

Finally putting him in his place feels so much better than I expected it would. It's as if I'm weightless, soaring through the air on a cloud. It feels damn good.

Tui links her arm through mine, giggling. "Girl, you did good!"

Susan grabs my other hand, leaning her cheek on my shoulder. "I'm so proud of you for standing up to him." She lifts her head and peers back down the hall. "But I wish you'd let me punch him. He deserves a good junk punch for that shit he was spewing."

I can't help but laugh, patting her hand. "Maybe next time."

We make it back out to where the party is still in full swing, my guests none the wiser as to what just went down. I scan the crowd, searching for Dallas, but he's nowhere in sight.

I find Tony and tap him on the shoulder. "Hey, have you seen Dallas anywhere?"

His smile falters as he puts his beer down and takes my arm, leading me to the side. "He, uh, left."

I laugh, swatting him on the arm. "Nice try. Where is he really?"

He clears his throat. "He really did leave."

What? "He left?" He nods. "Well, did he say where he was going?" *Or why he was leaving without saying goodbye?*

Tony rakes a hand through his hair. "He, uh, didn't say. He was on the phone, and then he just walked out. Sorry, Marianne."

There has to be some explanation for it. Dallas wouldn't just leave me, on my birthday, not without saying goodbye. Would he?

Or was Ernie right? Did he suddenly realise he was too good for me?

No. He wouldn't do that. Dallas is a good guy. I know he wouldn't do that to me.

I make my way to the door and step out into the parking lot, my heart plummeting into my stomach. His car is gone. Pulling my phone out, I flick him a message.

Marianne: Hey, where are you? Everything okay?

I wait for the tell-tale sign of a message being typed out, but there's nothing. No jumping dots, no sound.

"Told you he'd trade you in," Ernie taunts over my shoulder. "You're just not good enough."

I force a smile on my face before the tears fall. "You don't know what you're talking about. He'll be back."

"Face it, Marianne, he ran out on you on your birthday. He's not coming back."

I wheel around to face him. "What did you say to him?" I demand, poking a finger at his chest. "What did you do?"

He holds his hands up. "This one isn't on me, sweetheart. He left all on his own."

"Stop it! I know him, he wouldn't just leave for no reason. You had something to do with this." I shove him. "Why are you even here? Why can't you just let me be happy?"

"Marianne? What's going on?" Tui steps in between us.

"What's he done?" Susan spits from behind me. She pushes past and gets right in his face. "What did you do?"

He squares his shoulders, leering back. "I didn't *do* anything. It's not my fault her boyfriend got tired of her and left."

Tui's eyes search mine, sympathy all over her face. "He left?" I nod just as a tear slowly glides down my cheek. I swipe it away angrily.

"He had something to do with it. He had to. Dallas wouldn't just leave."

"I know he wouldn't. That guy has it bad for you. He loves you."

"He does," I whisper, trying to convince myself as much as her.

"If he loves you so much, why didn't he tell you he was leaving?" Ernie sneers, and then the unmistakable sound of flesh hitting flesh meets my ears.

"Jesus Christ that hurt!" Susan says as she waves her hand through the air, and I push past Tui to get to her.

"Yes, girl! About time someone gave it to him." Tui holds her hand up, and Susan slaps it with her good hand, a grin spreading across her face.

"Oh my god, Suz. Are you okay?" I reach for her hand and inspect it, ignoring the ranting from behind her.

"Is *she* okay? I'm the one with a bruised jaw!" Ernie bellows, his fists clenched at his sides.

"Bruised ego more like," Tui mutters.

I know I shouldn't find it amusing that my friend dished out vengeance on my behalf, especially when I've got other things to worry about, but I do. I find it extremely amusing, and a small smile graces my lips.

Taking her face in my hands, I press my forehead to hers. "I could kiss you right now, you beautiful, crazy woman. I love that you did that for me."

"Someone had to." She turns and eyeballs Ernie. "There's more where that came from too.

"How's your hand?"

"Hurts like a bitch, but damn it was worth it to see the look on his face." She grins, then grimaces when she tries to move her fingers. "I think it might be broken."

I open my mouth to joke that we know a doctor but stop myself, my smile disappearing as worry takes hold of me again.

Tui wraps her arm around my shoulders. "Don't worry about it. He'll be back. You'll see."

Chapter Thirty-six

He didn't come back.

No response to my message.

No call.

Nothing.

He just up and left me on my birthday with no explanation, and I don't know how to feel about that. Part of me wants to believe there's a good reason for his disappearance, but the rational side of me doesn't buy it. There's no excuse for running out without a single word and then ghosting me.

I barely slept last night, tossing and turning, replaying the evening for clues and coming up empty. As far as I can tell, I did nothing to warrant him leaving, and Ernie swears black and blue he had nothing to do with it. He may be a sack of shit, but Suz threatened to clock him again and his story never changed, so I believe him.

There's only one thing for it. I'm going to have to don my crazy girlfriend hat and go to the children's hospital. If there's one thing I know about him, it's that he would never let those children down.

"I'm sorry, Marianne, he's not here," Maggie says as she rounds the desk to meet me. Her eyes are red, and her cheeks are flushed, and I don't like what that could mean. She places her hand on my arm with a sympathetic look. "Why don't you come with me a minute?" She leads me down the corridor into an empty room and closes the door behind us.

My heart rate kicks up a notch, and I feel sick to my stomach. "Maggie? What's going on?" My hand flies to my mouth as I whisper, "Did something happen to him?"

Maggie shakes her head, taking my hands as she guides me to a seat and crouches in front of me. "No, honey, he's fine. Well, as fine as he can be." Her voice catches in her throat and she looks past my head, rolling her lips inwards as she composes herself. When her eyes turn to mine again, they're filled with sorrow. "I'm so sorry to tell you this, but Missy took a turn last night."

Her words are like a punch to the stomach. I fold in half, clutching my middle. Tears spring to my eyes as I shake my head, not wanting to hear any more. "No," I whisper. "No."

Maggie sniffles, nodding her head. "We did all that we could, but she didn't make it."

A keening noise fills the air, and it's only when I gasp for breath that I realise it's coming from me. I clutch at my chest, sucking in ragged breath after ragged breath as I mourn the little girl with eyes like saucers.

The little girl taken from this world far too soon. Just like Dallas's child was.

Oh God, Dallas.

My head jolts upright as I search Maggie's eyes. "Dallas?"

She shakes her head. "He wasn't here when it happened, but he knows. He was called last night."

And that's why he left.

I'd give anything to take it back, for there to be any other reason. I'd even take him breaking up with me if it meant Missy could still be here with her toothy grin and her blushing cheeks. My heart aches at the thought of never seeing her again. And even more so at what this must be doing to Dallas.

I need to see him.

I need to make sure he's okay.

But what if that's not what he wants? What if he doesn't want to see me?

"You should go to him," Maggie says as if reading my thoughts. "He was pretty cut up when he received the call last night. He'll need you, even if he isn't showing it."

"What do I even say to him?"

She pats my hand. "You don't have to say anything. Just be there for him." She pushes up off the floor, taking my hand. "Come on."

I nod, letting her pull me to my feet. When our eyes meet, it's like the damn breaks and I fall apart all over again. Maggie wraps her arms around me, rubbing her hand in slow circles across my back as I cling to her. "I know, honey. I know."

"It's just so unfair," I sob into her shoulder.

"It is, but you have to try to focus on the positives or it will eat you up inside."

"What positive could come from a sweet little girl dying?"

Maggie pulls back, wiping the tears from my cheeks. "She's no longer in any pain."

I hadn't thought of it that way. It might not ease the pain *I'm* feeling, but it eases my soul to know she's at peace now. She deserves to be in peace.

Pulling myself together, I follow Maggie back down to the nurses' station. The other nurse on duty takes one look at my puffy face and gives me an understanding smile. Missy no doubt touched the lives of all these women and men who grace these halls. I've no doubt in my mind she would've kept them entertained and brightened their days just that little bit more, as she had with mine.

"Would you like to see the other children before you go? I'm sure they'd welcome a familiar face right about now."

I glance towards the double doors leading to the children and instantly see the empty bed by the window. Another sob escapes my lips as I cast an eye across to the bed next to it, where Sarah is curled up in a ball, staring at the empty space. If it's even possible, my heart breaks a little more as I bear witness to her sadness. She shouldn't have to be alone right now, not when her best friend is gone.

My feet start moving before I even register what I'm doing. One step, two steps, three then four. I pause in the doorway, hearing soft sniffles and hiccups. Sarah turns her tear-filled eyes to me, and her little face crumples. I rush to her, sweeping her into my arms. "Oh, sweet girl, it's okay. I'm here."

Chapter thirty-seven

Exhausted and emotionally drained after spending two hours sitting with the children, I make my way to Dallas's, still unsure what I'm going to say, but knowing I need to be there for him. It had been tough seeing the children mourn the loss of their friend, but in a way, it was also therapeutic to sit with them, and I feel now more than ever is the time to be with those we love. Even if he can't see that.

I pull up outside his house and note the curtains are still drawn. Part of me wants to use it as an excuse to run for the hills, scared of what might lie ahead, but deep down, I know this is where I need to be right now. When he'd lost his wife and unborn child, he'd thrown himself into volunteering at the children's hospital, and I've no doubt the loss of Missy has sent him spiralling backwards, reopening wounds he'd fought so hard to close.

On shaky legs, I walk up to the door, listening for any sounds of life inside, but I'm met with only silence. My heart pounds in my chest as I knock lightly and step back, waiting.

Nothing.

I try the door, and it swings open to reveal a darkened entry and staircase.

"Dallas?" I call softly as I ease the door closed behind me. "It's me, Marianne." I walk towards the stairs, but something tells me he wouldn't have made it that far. On a hunch, I head for the bay window off the living room. The one with the bookshelves either side.

There, curled on his side, I find him sleeping with a frown marring his face. He's still wearing last night's clothes and clutched in his arms is a photo frame. I don't have to see it to know it's a picture of his wife, Clarissa. And even though I understand it, it still hurts to see him like this.

I inch closer, careful not to wake him as I grab the blanket from the floor. I drape it over his legs, then attempt to ease the frame from his hands, but he clutches it to him, his eyes opening wide.

"What are you doing?" he says, sitting up and rubbing his eyes.

"I'm sorry, I didn't mean to wake you. I was just trying to make you more comfortable." I gesture to the blanket.

"I can take care of myself."

Ouch.

"I know, I was just—"

"Why are you here?" he interrupts, kicking the blanket off and dropping his feet to the ground.

I swallow the lump in my throat, trying not to cry at the harsh way he's speaking to me. I know it's his grief talking, but it's hard to hear.

"I, um, wanted to make sure you were okay." My fingers twine together in front of me as I shuffle my feet. "Maggie told me what happened," I whisper as fresh tears for the little girl who stole my heart spring to my eyes. "I'm so sorry, Dallas. I know how much she meant to you." I hesitate before reaching out to him, wanting nothing more than to hold him in my arms and take some of the pain away. He lets me wrap my arms around him but doesn't reciprocate, instead turning his head to look out the gap between the curtains. I let my arms drop to my sides and take a step back. "What can I do?"

He shakes his head, bringing his hand up to rub his forehead. "Nothing."

I swallow the bitterness in his tone, brushing my hands against my thighs as I step towards the kitchen. "Have you eaten? I can make you something."

"No, thank you. I'm not hungry."

"Okay, um, would you like to—"

"I don't want to do anything, Marianne. There's nothing you or anyone else can do to make this better. I just want to be alone."

"Oh, um, if that's what you want…"

He turns to me with eyes that no longer sparkle or crinkle at the sides. "It's what I want."

"Okay, I guess I'll go then." I go to kiss him goodbye, but again he turns his head.

"Don't."

"Is everything… is everything okay?" He looks at me as if I'm a moron, and I rush on to say, "I mean, obviously I know it's not *okay*. It's devastating what happened. But I mean, is everything okay… with us?"

His eyes search mine, a frown marring his face. "No, it's not." He lets out a sigh, and my heart plummets into my stomach. "I can't do this anymore."

"You can't do what anymore?" I whisper even though I already know the answer.

"Us, Marianne. I can't do *us* anymore." His hand stretches across his forehead again, as if trying to rub away the pain.

"But why?" My lip trembles as I fight to keep it together.

"Because I can't take another person leaving me." His voice cracks as he turns his head away. I rush to kneel before him, taking his hands in mine.

"I'm not leaving you, Dallas, I promise. I love you."

He shakes his head, pulling his hands free. "You can't promise that. Things happen that are out of our control."

"Yes, they do, but that doesn't mean I'll ever leave."

"Maybe not willingly," he says softly, "but eventually you'll leave too. I'm just getting in first." He stands, walking towards the front door and holding it open.

"Dallas, please." A sob breaks free as I stand between him and the door. "Please, let me in. Let me show you I'm not going anywhere."

"I'm sorry, Marianne. I can't. I thought I could, but I can't."

I search his eyes but all I see is a man resigned to his fate. There's no changing his mind.

"Okay, I'll go, but only because you're asking me to, not because I want to." I step out the door and onto the landing. "But if you change your mind, I'm here, okay? I'll always be here for you, Dallas."

He nods but doesn't meet my eyes before the door is closed with a light click.

I manage to keep it together as I walk down the path to the safety of my car, but as soon as the door is shut, I crumble into a blubbering mess.

Chapter thirty-eight

"How're you doing, girl?" Tui asks as she flips the sign on the door to 'closed' and snibs the lock. Ever since my birthday a few weeks ago, Susan and I have been meeting here after work on a Friday for a coffee and catch up. I don't know what the girls get out of it, but it helps me keep my mind off things.

"I've been better, but I'm okay." And I am this time. After things went down with Ernie, I'd pushed everyone but Susan away and kept to myself, but this time around, I'm grateful to have both my friends by my side, keeping me grounded. "I went by his place after work the other day and left a container of lasagne on his porch." I shrug. "Still no word from him though."

"What's it been now? Three weeks?" Susan asks as she helps herself to a scroll from the cabinet.

"Mmhmm. Though it feels like longer."

"Have you tried calling him?" Tui asks, ambling around the counter to start on the coffees.

I shake my head. "No."

"Well, are you going to?"

"I hadn't planned on it. This is what he wanted. He told me to leave, remember?"

"And yet you're still dropping food around at his place every week." Tui folds her arms across her chest, raising a brow.

"Well, yeah, I can't just stop caring because he asked me to leave. I still want to make sure he's okay. I miss him."

"You don't have to tell us that, girl. But maybe you need to tell *him*."

"I did." I throw my hands up in exasperation. "I told him I was always here if he needed me, and I know he knows it's me delivering food. Doesn't that prove I still care?"

"To us, yeah," Susan says, "but he's a man, and sometimes they need to have things spelled out for them." She pours an obscene amount of sugar into her coffee. "Take Gus for example. I've lost count how many times I've shown him that *365 Days* movie, and he *still* doesn't get that I like it rough sometimes." She shakes her head. "Sometimes actions just don't speak louder than words."

Tui stares at her with her mouth agape. "Three words. Too much information." She shudders. "But, and I can't believe I'm saying this, maybe Suz is right."

Susan pulls a chunk off her scroll and tosses it at Tui. "It's been known to happen on occasion. Don't act so surprised."

"Look, all I'm saying is, what's the harm in sending him a message or stopping by his place? It's easy to pretend you can live without someone when they're not there reminding you how much you need them."

"I guess."

"And what's the worst that can happen? He sends you away again? At least then you know where you stand, and you can move on."

"I don't want to move on though," I say softly. "I'm not ready to let him go. Not when I've only just found him."

Susan wraps her arm around me and leans her head on my shoulder. "You won't have to move on. He'll come around. That man is so in love with you, it's sickening."

"She's not wrong."

Susan feigns shock. "Twice in one day? Who'd have thought?" She turns to me with a glint in her eyes. "You know what you need to do? You need to pull off one of those grand gesture things like in those cheesy movies you two love so much."

"You think that would work?"

"It always works in the movies, doesn't it?"

"I guess."

"So, what are our options?" She gestures to Tui for a sheet of paper and a pen.

"Unless it's punching Biff to save his virtue, I really have no clue," I say with a shrug.

"I'm not even going to pretend I know what you're talking about. What's his favourite movie?"

I roll my eyes. "*Back to the Future*. That's the big gesture in that movie. George McFly punches Biff to protect his future wife."

Susan screws her nose up, pointing her pen at me. "The fact you even know that should be proof enough you're meant to be together." She paces back and forth, tapping the pen to her chin. "Oh my God, I've got it!" She runs around to the cabinet, giggling. Pulling out two bread rolls, she holds them either side of her head. In a breathy voice, she says, "Help me, Doc Mahoney, you're my only hope."

"You realise that's *Star Wars,* right?" Tui says through her laughter.

"Of course I do," Susan snaps. "It's just as cheesy as *Back to the Future.* Plus, *all* the guys our age love Princess Leia. She's like every guy's wet dream."

"Right, but where's the grand gesture in that?"

She looks at me incredulously. "Uh, hello? You'd be getting your kit off and walking around with donuts on your ears. I think that's grand gesture enough, don't you?" She snorts, taking a bite of one of the rolls.

"I don't know…"

"Come on, admit it, that's gold! And I don't see anyone else coming up with any ideas." She folds her arms across her chest, raising her brow in challenge. "Tui?"

Tui shakes her head, holding her hands in the air. "Don't look at me."

"Well then, it's settled. Tomorrow morning, we go find you a gold bikini."

Chapter thirty-nine

"Are you sure about this?" I ask, smoothing the gold lamé fabric of my pants beneath my fingers.

"Uh, no. No, I'm not," Susan scoffs from the backseat. "I can't believe you're going through with it." Tui levels her with a glare in the rearview mirror, and she sighs. "But I guess it's kinda cool."

"I look ridiculous, don't I?"

"Well…"

"I think you look cute, girl. He won't be able to resist your charms."

Susan snorts. "He can't even *see* her charms under that hideous shirt."

I look down at the orange and blue striped shirt with purple suspenders over top and can't help but giggle. It really is hideous, but it's all they had at the costume hire place.

We'd gone in search of the famed gold bikini, but when I'd laid eyes on the oversized gold pants with purple suspenders, I knew what I needed to do.

"Have you got the music ready?"

Tui wiggles her phone in the air. "All cued up and ready to go."

"Okay." I huff out a breath, then swing the door open and jump out before I can change my mind. I give her the nod, then awkwardly run up the path as my floppy shoes flap against the ground. Circus music booms from the car speakers as I dance around the lawn, kicking my legs out and pumping my arms up and down.

The curtain of the living room twitches, so I ramp it up even more. Pulling out a set of juggling balls, I begin throwing them in the air and attempting to catch them. The neighbour comes out and stands by the fence, grinning and giving me the thumbs up as I continue making a fool of myself.

I pull out every trick I've ever seen Dallas do for the children and even add in a few of my own. More people come out to watch, and a group of kids hang over the fence, clapping and laughing. Even Susan gets into it, hooting and wolf whistling as I pull a never-ending hanky from my pocket.

As the song draws to an end, I start to question where I go from here. I glance behind me for guidance from the girls, who both roll their hands in the *keep going* motion. So, I do. I dance and clown around for two full songs before the door opens and Dallas steps out onto the landing.

The music dies down and everyone seems to melt into the background as I pull off the ghastly wig and cautiously make my way over to him. His expression is unreadable, and it has my heart pounding in my chest.

He leans against the veranda column, crossing his feet at his ankles. "What's all this about?"

"You have dedicated your life to helping others. Even in the toughest time of your life, you chose to share the joy of laughter with those children, and it means the world to them, Dallas. To them, their families, the nurses… and to me," I add softly. "I know Missy passing was a horrible blow. It was for me too. But I also know she wouldn't want you to forget the good times. She would want you to find the joy again." I throw my hands out to the side. "I just want you to be happy. And I know that's hard right now, but I could help to make it easier. I could lighten the load for you, Dallas."

"By acting the clown?"

"If that's what it takes, yes."

The corner of his mouth ticks up in the hint of a smile. "And what if I wanted you to strut around like that every day for the next year?"

I tug at the too-big pants. "Then I'd need to actually purchase the suit. Hire fees are exorbitant." I grin. "Whatever it takes though, I'll do it. I want you in my life, Dallas. For better, for worse, in sickness and in health. I'm going to be here every step of the way. You can't get rid of me."

"It's a good thing I don't want to get rid of you then, isn't it?"

"You don't?"

"Nope." He shakes his head, walking down the steps towards me.

"Well that was easier than I thought it'd be."

"Honestly, I've been kicking myself the last few weeks for what I said to you. I never should've told you to leave."

"It's okay."

"No, it's not. I did a shitty thing by walking out on you. In my head, I thought I was saving you the heartache, but really, I was just being selfish. I needed time to be by myself." He runs a hand over the scruff on his chin. "At least, I thought I did. But once I realised my mistake, it was too late. You were already gone, and I couldn't make myself pick up the phone." He chuckles. "You did me a favour by coming here."

"So, that whole…" I swirl a finger through the air where I'd been clowning around. "I didn't need to do that?"

"Nope."

I slap a hand on his arm playfully. "Then why didn't you stop me?"

"Well, you'd already started, and you'd clearly gone to a lot of trouble…" I fold my arms across my chest, pursing my lips, and he laughs. "It really was very good. If that whole bakery thing doesn't pan out, any circus would be lucky to have you." He grins, and damn it all, I can't help but grin back.

"I was pretty good, wasn't I?"

"The best." He wraps his arms around my waist, his eyes crinkling as he beams at me.

"And there it is," I sigh. "That 1.21 gigawatt smile I love so much."

"I don't think that's—"

I cut him off with my finger on his lips. "Just shut up and kiss me."

Epilogue
three years later

"Dallas, Marianne." Maggie greets us with a hug. "And this must be Toby." She crouches down, offering her hand to the newest addition to our family. "Hi, I'm Maggie."

Toby steps out from around my legs and gives her a shy smile before sliding his pudgy fingers into hers. "Hi."

"Your mum and dad are pretty famous around here, did you know that?"

He peers up at me with those big brown eyes of his and toothy grin. "Really?"

"Oh yeah. The children love them." Maggie puts her hand up to her lips, whispering, "I think it's because they dress so silly. What do you think?"

Toby giggles, his eyes flicking to our brightly coloured wigs and outfits then back to Maggie. He nods. "Yeah, they are silly."

"Come on, squirt. I'll introduce you to the kids." Dallas takes his hand and leads him through the double doors, while Maggie and I watch.

"So, how's it all going? He settling in okay?"

"Yeah, I think so. He's still getting used to us, but he seems pretty happy."

She reaches out, rubbing a hand up and down my arm. "How could he not be? You two were made to be parents."

"Thanks. It's not something I ever thought I'd do until I met Dallas." I grin as I watch him leaping about with Toby in his arms. "He's a natural."

"He is. And Toby seems smitten with the both of you already."

"You think so? I keep feeling like I'm mucking everything up."

Maggie chuckles. "Welcome to the world of parenthood, my friend. No one really knows what they're doing. We all just make it up as we go along."

"Oh great. Remind me why I signed up for this again?" I grin, nudging her with my elbow.

"Because that little boy needed parents, and your man over there needed a child. You'll get the hang of it, I promise."

"I hope so."

"I know so." She turns to the desk, grabbing a chart and tucking it under her arm. "Hey, isn't today the big opening?"

"Yeah, it is. Once we're finished up here, it's show time." I wiggle my fingers in the air like I'm on a Broadway show. "It's been a hard road, but we're finally ready for it." I raise a hand to my hair, patting it. "You can't tell, but under here is a whole heap more greys. But I'm kinda digging it." I grin.

"Well, unlike the rest of us, you can pull off any look." She gestures at my costume. "Case and point."

"What? This old thing?" I run my hand over my dungarees, and Maggie shakes her head with a grin.

"I've got to get back to my rounds, but if I don't see you before, good luck with it. I'll try and pop in on my way home."

"Thanks, Maggie." I watch her leave then turn to my two favourite boys and dance toward them to join in the fun.

###

"Relax, Marianne, you've got this." Dallas's hands on my shoulders offer a semblance of calm, and I allow myself a moment to stop and take it in before the chaos begins.

This is it.

The day is finally here. Two years of full-time study, one year of work experience with Tui, and I'm finally here, where I've always dreamed of being; in my very own boutique bakery. It's just as I pictured it, with bare wooden floors, couches and cushions in the corner, local artists' paintings adorning the walls, a deep woodfire oven to bake the bread in, and an open-style kitchen where customers can witness the magic as it happens.

"Almost show time!" Susan calls as she saunters in through the back. "How are the nerves? I thought you might need this." She plonks a bottle of wine on the bench in front of me. "Hey, squirt." She ruffles Toby's hair.

"Oh my God, Suz, I could kiss you!" I grab her by the shoulders and pull her in quickly. "I'm so bloody nervous it's not funny."

"Uh, no language in front of the kid." She places her hands over Toby's ears.

"Sorry, I'm just nervous, I've put everything into this."

"I knew you'd be overthinking it." She shakes her head as she lets go of Toby, then grabs my hand and drags me through to the front. With her hands on my shoulders, she pushes me forward. "Take a look around."

I let my eyes rove over the tables and chairs, the couches and cushions.

"You did this. You made this happen. *You*, Marianne. And I'm so stinking proud of you."

Tears well as I grin at her. "It's a good thing I stopped wearing makeup or I'd have mascara running down my face about now." I lean my head on her shoulder. "It *is* a pretty cool space."

"*So* cool, and the best part is, I know the owner, so I get first dibs on everything."

"Oh, is that right?"

"Yeah, I mean, it's in the best friend's handbook. 'Thou shalt giveth thy friend all the food' or some such."

"You want another cronut, don't you?"

She nods her head. "You know I do."

I flick my head towards the far cabinet. "Knock yourself out. Just make sure you leave some for *paying* customers too."

She claps in glee then darts around me. "I believe the term is finders keepers, and I found you *way* before anyone else did. These babies are mine."

"Marianne? Can I borrow you for a sec?" Dallas stands by my very first purchase for the bakery; my KitchenAid mixer. "I know we only have a few minutes until opening, but I wanted to give you something first." He pulls three frames out from behind his back, placing them on the counter. "I thought you could hang them in here somewhere."

Fresh tears spring to my eyes as I run my fingers over the photo we'd taken just the other day. Dallas, Toby and I standing outside the front doors pointing up at the sign. Next to that is the certificate I received when I graduated, now residing in a beautifully rustic frame to match the decor. Beside that is a picture I've not seen before, but one he must've taken all those years ago when he convinced me to invest in my future and buy the mixer. I'm standing in front of the wall of mixers with my finger against my chin, and I have the biggest smile on my face.

"I knew it was an important moment for you, and I wanted to commemorate it for you."

Throwing my arms around his neck, I squeeze him tight. "Thank you, I love them. I love *you*." I plant a kiss on his lips. "I know exactly where I'm going to put them too." I tug him out to the front with me. "I was going to surprise you, but now seems as good a time as any." In the corner by the window, there are two couches and a group of scatter cushions. There's a small bookshelf below the window, and sitting on top is a small painted sign that reads, "Missy's Corner" with one of her scarves folded across the corner.

"Marianne," Dallas whispers as he takes it all in.

"I hope it's okay. I wanted to do something in her memory."

"It's beautiful."

"And see here?" I point to the bare brick space above one of the couches. "I was saving this spot for a large piece from the gallery down the road, but I think I'd like to hang those frames you gave me here instead."

"Perfect."

"One minute to go!" Susan calls out as she pours the wine into glasses and hands us each one. "This is quite exciting. Have you seen how many people are out there?"

"I… no…" I turn back to the window and actually look outside this time. "Oh my God," I whisper as I stare at the many people lined up outside my bakery. I turn to Susan with a look of shock. "How many do you think are out there?"

She scoots closer to the window and cranes her neck. "Easily twenty, maybe more. It goes right around the corner."

"Are you serious?" I screech, pushing her out of the way to look for myself.

"It's time, Marianne," Dallas says as he points to his watch with a smile. "You ready?"

"I guess I have to be, don't I?" I giggle, downing the glass of wine and handing it back to Susan before brushing my hands down my apron front. "You girls ready?" I ask Beth and Hayley, my new apprentice and shop assistant. They each nod, giving me a thumbs up. "Here goes nothing."

On shaky legs, I make my way to the door, and unsnib the lock, then flip the sign on the door to 'open'. I swing the door inwards and attach it to the hook on the wall, then step outside to greet everyone.

Before I can even speak, I'm nearly bowled over by Tui launching herself at me. "You did it! I'm so proud of you, girl!"

"Tui, you goon, what are you doing lined up out here?"

"Wasn't about to let anyone else be the first in line for your big day. I'm your biggest fan, you know." She puffs her chest out. "And it's a good thing I got here early too. I had this one trying to beat me to it." She nods behind her, and Daniel winks at me.

"I'm the official taste-tester, so it's only right I'm in there first. Isn't that right, Marianne?"

I can't help but grin at these two. "I'm afraid to say, Suz bet you to it." I hook a thumb over my shoulder to where Susan is standing with yet another cronut in her hand.

"What?" she calls out with cream on her lips. "It's called quality control."

"Sure it is." I step around my friends to address the crowd of people. "Welcome to Deep Heated, the boutique bakery for all your pastry needs. I'm Marianne Mahoney, the pastry chef and owner. If there's anything you need made to order, I'm happy to help. Enjoy!" I step back, waving my arm towards the door. Tui and

Daniel disappear inside alongside everyone else, while I stand back and watch with a satisfied grin on my face.

"You did it," Dallas says as he joins me out front, wrapping his arm around my shoulders and staring up at the sign above the door. "I still can't believe you called it that." He chuckles, and my grin stretches across my face.

"It's what brought us together."

"I still think it should've been called Marianne's Moist Morsels," Susan says as she licks cream from her fingers.

"First of all, eww." I screw my nose up. "And second of all, this has more meaning to it. More of a personal touch to it."

"I don't know. You have to be pretty personal to get *moist*." She draws the word out, making me cringe.

"Ugh, don't. It's right up there with the word *girlfriend*." I shudder, and Dallas pulls me into his side, chuckling.

"I seem to recall you getting used to the word after a while."

"Only because I was angling for another word," I tease, holding my ring finger out in front of us. I snuggle into his side, resting my head on his shoulder.

"Ugh." Susan mimes putting her finger down her throat. "You two are so sickly sweet sometimes."

"Says the woman about to walk down the aisle herself in a few weeks."

"Yeah, but you won't see me all goo-goo eyed. I'll be strutting down the aisle to Miss Queen B herself." She breaks off into a rendition of *Single Ladies* complete with hair flicks and arm pumping action.

"I wouldn't expect anything less."

"Um, Marianne?" Beth pops her head out the door. "There's someone requesting you for a catering job?"

"I'll be right there." I turn in Dallas's arms, my fingers threading through the hair at the base of his neck as I grin up at him. "Whoa, this is heavy, doc."

"Nothing you can't handle, madam chef."

"Oh, I know." My lips curl into a smile before pressing to his. "I've got this."

A Note From the Author

Thank you so much for taking the time to read Deep Heat! It was originally a short for an anthology, but I just fell in love with the characters and had to take the story further. I'm so stoked to finally be able to share Dallas and Marianne with you!

Hopefully you enjoyed reading it as much as I enjoyed writing it. If you did, I would love it if you could leave a review. Reviews not only help our work to be seen, they also offer valuable feedback.

If you would like to keep up to date with my releases, please feel free to sign up to my newsletter. I promise, I won't spam you!

Once again, thank you for reading!

Stacey xxx

Newsletter sign-up: http://eepurl.com/cULu_f

Acknowledgements

First, I'd like to start by thanking you, the reader, for picking up my book! I hope you enjoyed it. It was a fun story to come up with, even if it made me pull my hair out once or twice through the process!

To my girl, Trina, for always having my back when it comes to my writing, listening to me whinge and promise it will be done a million times before it's actually done, and making sure I don't sound stupid. Love you!

To Debs, for encouraging me to keep going even when I wanted to give up, and for being a constant inspiration. One day I'm going to write a twisted short story that will knock your socks off like yours do to me. Every. Single. Time.

To my reader group, Broadbent's Bookish Babes, thanks for all the support throughout the years, guys! I love you all!

To my children, who let me sneak off to the office to write, and to my husband who kept them entertained while I did, I love you guys xxx

About the Author

Stacey lives in Ashburton, New Zealand, with her husband and three children. An avid reader and self-confessed book-a-holic, she has always had a love of the written word, so it was only a matter of time before she took pen to paper and began on her writing journey. Stacey is a multi-genre author, with books from light-hearted comedies to zombie thrillers to contemporary romance. You can often find her lurking on social media so don't be afraid to reach out and have a chat.

www.staceybroadbent.com

Other Books by Stacey Broadbent

Standalone
Never Judge a Book
Emma
Fever
A Christmas Tail
Broken

Hellhound MC series
Cut Loose
Break Loose
Let Loose (coming soon)

A Step in Time series
Dancing through the Storm
Dancing in Circles
Dancing with Destiny
A Step in Time: the complete series

Dark sins series
Sins of the Flesh
Mine

Super Mum series
Frazzled
Frazzled and Frumpy
Frazzled, Frumpy, and Fabulous!
Super Mum: the complete series

Short Stories and Poetry
Musings, Mournings, and Misadventures
Musings, Mayhem, and Mystery
Musings, Magic, and Mischief

Anthologies
Scars to your Beautiful
Witching Hour: Vices and Virtues
The White Ribbon Collection
A Touch of Inspiration
No Place Like Home
Hellhounds
Serendipity
Lucky Star

9 780473 531188